# Kiss Kiss,
# Bang Bang

# Kiss Kiss,
# Bang Bang

*Ashley & JaQuavis*

www.urbanbooks.net

Urban Books, LLC
97 N18th Street
Wyandanch, NY 11798

ISBN 13: 978-1-62286-980-0
ISBN 10: 1-62286-980-X

First Mass Market Printing April 2012
First Trade Paperback Printing November 2010
Printed in the United States of America

10 9 8 7 6 5 4 3

*This is a work of fiction. Any references or similarities to actual events, real people, living, or dead, or to real locales are intended to give the novel a sense of reality. Any similarity in other names, characters, places, and incidents is entirely coincidental.*

Distributed by Kensington Publishing Corp.
Submit Orders to:
Customer Service
400 Hahn Road
Westminster, MD 21157-4627
Phone: 1-800-733-3000
Fax: 1-800-659-2436

# Prologue

I can't wait until you come home
I miss you
Don't be wild'n out in Vegas, nigga
I don't want to have to fuck a bitch up

Love always,
Six

Free smirked and shook his head when he read the text message from his girlfriend of seven years. Six had been his backbone since he was twenty years old, and they had experienced plenty of ups and downs together. Although he loved Six to his core, in the past he had hurt her more than once with his cheating ways. He was young when they had first met, and it had taken him awhile to learn how to be a good man to her, but from the first day he saw her, he knew that she would be wifey. He knew that Six wasn't making idle threats either. She had fucked up a couple chicks over him. The last time she caught him cheating, she had beaten a girl so badly that the girl was hospitalized for days. That had been over a year ago, and needless to say, no other chick in Wayne County had tried to come at Free since. Everybody knew what was up, Free was taken, and from that point on, he had been faithful. "She always thinking something," he mumbled to himself as he pulled the small velvet box that contained the two-karat engagement ring that he planned on surprising her with. Six really didn't know how much Free had grown. He was ready to make it official. He knew that no other woman could hold him down the way that Six could, and he was ready to make an honest woman out of her.

"You really gon' ask her to marry you, huh?" Big Lou asked with a skeptical look on his face.

"Yeah, man. She's getting antsy and shit. She been tripping on me lately, doubting me and all that. She keeps bringing up the past. She talking like I don't love her. She still thinks that I'm on the same ol' shit."

"Nah, fam. Six knows what's up. Y'all have been through a lot together. You would kill a nigga for her," Big Lou replied as his New York accent oozed off of every word.

"Yeah, I got a good woman. It's about time I settled down with her. I'm just trying to make her happy, man."

Big Lou cracked a smile as he shook his head from side to side.

"What, nigga?" Free asked with a look of irritation on his face. He was trying to keep it funky with Big Lou because he wanted an honest opinion regarding what he was about to do.

"I never thought I would see the day when young Alfree would be ready to settle down with one chick," Big Lou responded in disbelief.

"Don't be calling me Alfree," Free said. He hated his government name and had shortened it to Free a long time ago. He fumbled with the ring box, opening and closing it repeatedly as he felt the plane prepare for its landing. "She deserves this yo. Those other chicks can't do shit for me."

"What about that bitch Asia? Shorty got a fat ass! You gon' give all that up? Because I'll step in and hit that since you gon' be a one-woman man now. I'll give her some of this King Kong," Big Lou stated with laughter in his voice.

Free shook his head and replied, "Man, go for what you know. She do have the goods though, but I don't love them hoes. The only one who matter is Six."

"Six is a good chick. I ain't ever met a woman like her. She a gangsta too. Congratulations, man," Big Lou stated in a genuine tone.

"Thanks," Free replied as he rested his head against the leather first-class seats. He closed his eyes and thought back to

*Seven Years Ago in NYC*

The club filled quickly as New York's elite walked through the door and prepared to celebrate New Year's Eve. Everybody who was anybody came out to bring in 2002 with Twin and his entourage. Twin was the most successful party promoter in the city, and he threw the biggest parties and invited all the boroughs. Free and Big Lou pulled up to the crowded club as they watched the line wrap around the corner.

"Damn, nigga! It's jumping in that joint," Big Lou stated as he took the safety off his automatic pistol.

"Good," Free replied as he loaded his .45-caliber pistol with a full clip. He parked his black-on-black Navigator at the side of the busy street, and both men concealed the burners in their waistlines as they exited the vehicle. They walked up to the crowded club and headed toward the front of the line as they prepared to step into the club. They had no intentions of standing in the line. Big Lou had gotten them hooked up with VIP passes, so they didn't have to wait. Partygoers complained as they watched Free and Big Lou disregard the entire line.

"Hold up, homeboy," a big bodybuilder-type bouncer said as he held his hand up to stop the two from entering the building. "Y'all see that line back there?" he asked. "Unless y'all got VIP passes, y'all gon' have to wait just like everybody else."

Big Lou pulled two orange-colored, laminated passes that had *VIP* stamped on the front.

The bouncer chuckled and said, "Those ain't gon' get you up in here. Those passes are from last night's event. They ain't even the right color."

"What? My man gave me these. What color they supposed to be?" Big Lou asked, getting heated that the bouncer was trying to chump him in front of the crowd of people gathered by the door.

"The only color that matter is green, nigga," Free interrupted as he placed a knot of hundred-dollar bills in the bouncer's hand.

"True," the bouncer replied as he lifted the red velvet rope and let them into the club without even searching them.

"I'ma kill that mu'fuckin' crackhead that sold me those damn passes," Big Lou stated as they made their way to the bar.

"Don't worry about it. It's nothing. We about to get all that cake from the door. That money coming right back to me," Free stated. Free and Big Lou sat back and enjoyed the party as they waited for the guest of honor to arrive. Free checked his cell phone and noted that it was only ten o'clock. The inside of the club was already packed and there were hundreds of people still waiting outside to get in. Free's eyes scanned the room until he found the sign displayed above the door that displayed the maximum occupancy. *This nigga is cleaning the fuck up. He charging fifty a head and this mu'fucka can hold a thousand people. That's fifty stacks. Easy money,* Free thought as he felt the cold steel that rested against his hip, ensuring that it was there if he should need to use it. Big Lou made the most of his time and entertained a group of women, but Free stayed focused, clocking each and every dollar that came into the club as he waited patiently for his plan to pop off.

"It's showtime, kid," Big Lou leaned over and whispered in Free's ear as they both watched Twin and his entourage enter.

"There go that bitch Twin fucking with. She ain't all that!" one of the girls said as they spit venom on the girl who walked in on Twin's arm.

Free and Big Lou focused their attention on the brown-skinned female that had entered the club with Twin. The silk Lela Rose minidress that she wore rested perfectly on her five feet seven inch frame, showing off her thick thighs and long legs. Her body glistened a healthy glow that matched her green eyes that were obviously contacts, but she rocked them well. Her hair flowed loosely, but was pulled to one side and stopped right above her perky breast line. She was perfect from the top of her head to the bottom of her French-manicured toes and to top it off, Twin was holding onto her waist as if her pussy was laced in gold. Envious vibes spread through the room instantly as every man wished he was in Twin's shoes, and every woman wanted to be whoever the girl was. Her name instantly became "that bitch" as girls who were normally confident became insecure in their own skin.

"Damn," was all that Free and Big Lou could say as their eyes followed the woman's ass as she stepped up the stairs that led to the VIP lounge. Any other day Free would have made it a point to step to her, but today he was on business.

"Keep your eye on the money," Free stated as he watched the door. From the bar, they had a clear view of almost every angle in the club. They could even see Twin and his entourage through the clear glass of the upstairs VIP window. Free smiled as he watched money continue to flow through the door. Once the club reached its maximum occupancy, a huge smile spread across Free's face. He checked the time again. "Ten minutes to midnight," he said to himself as he watched Twin make his way from the VIP room to the DJ booth.

"What's good, New York?" Twin asked as he took the microphone. He had a bottle of Cristal in one hand and the microphone in the other. "I want to thank all y'all mu'fuckas for coming through and bringing the New Year in right with your boy."

Free smiled as he listened to Twin's slurred speech. It was obvious that he was drunk. Twin wasn't pissy, but Free knew that he had consumed enough liquor to knock him off his square. He reached for the girl who had entered the club with him and pulled her up into the DJ's booth. "Now everybody grab your lady and grab a glass of champagne so we can count it down," he said.

"Ten, nine, eight, seven, six, five, four, three, two, one—Happy New Year!" Twin poured Cristal into his mouth straight from the bottle and then kissed his girl sloppily on the lips. "Now let's keep this shit going," he yelled into the microphone.

Everybody resumed their party antics . . . everyone except for Free and Big Lou. They watched Twin closely. He leaned into the girl's ear and said, "Go collect my money and take it to the back." Twin didn't realize that he still had the microphone in his hand. Everyone was too busy to notice the comment, but Free picked up on it.

"Go toward the bathroom and wait for the bitch to come back there," Free instructed. Big Lou nodded and made his way to the back of the club. Free's eyes watched intently as the girl went to the door. She was handed a backpack full of money. She then made her way to the bar and collected from there as well. *This nigga getting paid from the bar too!* Free thought to himself as dollar signs filled his eyes.

He looked up toward the VIP where Twin had the crowd captivated as he threw dollar bills into the air, making it rain on the crowd. He was flashing his cash. It was obvious that Twin wanted everybody to know he was paid.

*Yeah, I see you, nigga,* Free thought to himself.

He refocused his attention on the girl who was collecting Twin's money. He let her step a couple feet in front of him so that it would not be obvious that he was tailing her, and then he discreetly followed her down the dark, narrow hallway. When they were halfway down the hall, Free looked back to make sure the coast was clear and then pulled his .45 from his waist and grabbed the girl from behind. He put his hand over her mouth and pulled her into an empty office where Big Lou was already waiting.

"Listen . . . I'm not trying to hurt you. Don't scream; if you do, you ain't gon' leave me no choice. I'm just here for the money. Do you understand?" Free asked in a low voice as he whispered in her ear.

The girl nodded her head, and Free removed his hand from her mouth.

"Give me the money," Big Lou said as he roughly snatched the backpack away from her.

"Y'all niggas must really have a death wish," she said as she shook her head from side to side. She sucked her teeth and shifted her weight to one leg.

"What?" Free asked.

"You really think you about to make it out of this club with that cash? You must not know how Twin got his nickname. That nigga keep the twin desert eagles on him. You mu'fuckas ain't gon' make it three feet out this door before he put them to use."

Free grinned at the girl's attitude.

"You think yo' nigga big shit, huh? He's a pussy. I'll put something hot in his ass. Don't think ya' boy the only one with heat," Free threatened.

"Man, don't listen to this bitch. That nigga is drunk. He won't know what hit him until it's too late," Big Lou stated. They prepared to open the door to leave.

"All right, take your asses out there and get popped if you want to. He got four niggas watching each door with the pistols already locked and loaded. Twin ain't stupid. He knew somebody was gon' try to flex tonight. He is waiting to twist a nigga cap back. Ain't nobody walking out of here with them backpacks tonight. How does it feel to be fucked?"

"Stop flapping yo' dick, suckers," Big Lou stated as he chuckled at his own joke.

"Okay . . . go ahead. Go for what you know, but you ain't getting out of here tonight, at least not walking with that backpack in your hands. I take it that was your only reason for coming. So tell me, how does it feel to be fucked?"

Big Lou got heated and pushed the girl against the wall. He pointed his pistol in her face and said, "Look, you smart mouth bitch!"

Free was sure that Big Lou would put fear in the girl's heart. His six feet four inch frame and

280 pounds intimidated most people, but to his surprise, the girl didn't flinch.

"No, you look, nigga. The way I see it, you got one of two choices. You can either get laid out in this mu'fucka and get carried out in bags, or you can put me on, give me a cut, and I'll carry that bag out for you."

Big Lou released her neck and looked at Free, who was contemplating the situation.

"You Twin's bitch. You were just parading around here on his arm. Why would you help us? How I know you ain't setting us up?" Free asked suspiciously.

"A *bitch* like money," she replied, enunciating the word bitch to let him know she didn't appreciate being called out of her name.

"Fuck it. What you got in mind?"


Big Lou walked out of the room and walked directly up the VIP area. "Hold up. You ain't got a pass, so you can't get in," a bouncer said as he noticed that Big Lou wasn't wearing a VIP tag. Big Lou immediately got loud, causing a scene.

"Man, fuck all that! I paid money just like the rest of these niggas. Why I can't get in there? That's where the party at."

"You ain't got a tag, so you ain't getting in!" the bouncer said more forcefully this time. Big Lou threw a punch that knocked the bouncer out cold. He pulled his gun and started waving it in the air wildly. He fired a single shot into the air, causing pandemonium to erupt throughout the club. It was the perfect distraction. Then he ducked low as he bobbed and weaved, maneuvering his way through the crowd of bodies toward the front door.

"That's our cue," the girl said as she heard the screams inside the club. She ran out the back door. One of Twin's guards stopped her on her way out. "Yo, ma, where you going? You straight? You got Twin's money?"

"Yeah, I got it. Hurry up, get in there, somebody's shooting. You got to get Twin out of there," she said in a panicked voice as she put the backpack on her back.

"Wait outside while we clear this shit out," the bouncer replied as he pulled his gun and made his way into the club. She ran to her car and popped her trunk as she hurriedly placed the backpack inside.

"What you doing, ma? Give me the bag," Free said eagerly as he looked from left to right.

"Nigga, you ain't gon' get ghost on me. I'll meet you at Junior's tomorrow at noon. I'll bring

the money with me; we'll split it up then. Now go
before Twin sees you."

"Don't fuck with me, shorty," Free stated in a
hushed tone as he grabbed her arm tightly.

"Look, I said I got you. Now go!"

Free reluctantly ran toward his car.

"Where the dough?" Big Lou asked as soon as
Free got in.

"The bitch got it," Free replied. "She gon' meet
me tomorrow, and we gon' split it up then."

"How you know she gon' show up?"

Free looked out his window as he watched Twin
run out to the girl. She instantly began to cry and
her act was so realistic that he had to let out a
laugh. "She'll show."

The next day Free waited anxiously in the back
of the restaurant as he watched the girl approach.
She was wearing an all-white Versace sundress,
and her hair was pulled back off her face in a loose
ponytail. The side of her face was swollen, and her
lip was busted. She carried the backpack at her
side as she limped toward him. Pain was written
all over her face with each step that she took.

"Here's the money," she said.

"What happened to your face?" Free asked her
as he watched her sit down tenderly, trying to
avoid causing herself any further pain.

"I took an ass-whooping for forty grand," she replied nonchalantly as if it were no big deal.

Free couldn't help but to laugh at the girl before him. She was unlike any chick that he had ever encountered. He was intrigued by her arrogant swagger, and her beauty was comparable to none.

"Let's go, shorty," he said as he stood up and took the backpack from her hands.

"Go where? I got to get my cut so I can get back before Twin notices I'm gone," she said.

"Fuck that nigga," Free said as he stood up and stared down at her. "You rolling with me."

"Excuse you? How you know I'm trying to fuck with you like that?" the girl replied with much attitude as she placed her hands on her hips.

"Don't front, ma. You wouldn't have let me get out of that club with your boy's cash if you weren't feeling a nigga."

A smile involuntarily graced her lips as she put her Dior sunglasses on her face to hide her true feelings. "I don't even know you," she replied sweetly, keeping up her hard exterior and playing hard to get.

"I'm Free," he replied as he held out his hand and turned to leave. "What's your name, ma?"

"Six," she hesitantly replied as she placed her hand in his and shook her head in doubt.

"Now you know me," Free said as he led her to his car.

"This is crazy," she told herself as she reluctantly followed behind him. "Twin will come after me."

"Listen, shorty, I'm not gon' let nobody harm you. All you got to do is keep it real with me. If you hold me down, I'll hold you down, a'ight?"

"Yeah, a'ight," Six replied with a seductive smile. "But can we leave town?"

Free stopped walking and looked Six directly in her eyes. "This nigga got you shook?"

"No, it's not that. I just want us to start fresh. A new city, a new beginning."

"Okay . . . but my man Big Lou coming with us." He wrapped his arm around her shoulders and then playfully pulled her to the car. It didn't matter that he didn't know Six from the next chick on the street. Free was a spontaneous person and blew wherever the wind took him. He chased the money, and as he walked toward his car, he chuckled thinking that he may have just met his match. "Where to?" he asked as he started his car.

"The Midwest," she replied. "I've got a father in Detroit. I haven't seen him since my mom died a few years ago."

When Free pulled away from the curb that day they became partners. Partners in crime, partners in life, partners in love. Everything was fifty-fifty with them. It was the beginning of the end.


Free opened his eyes when he felt the plane touch down in Detroit. He smiled as he reflected on the first time he had met Six. Just thinking about her made him love her more. As a man he felt like he was getting ready to give up a part of himself by marrying Six. Although he loved her more than life, and he planned to be with her, there was something about putting a ring on her finger that scared him. He had been planning this for some time now. For seven years he had been on his grind, trying to stack his chips so that he would be able to provide for himself and his woman. Six was spoiled. She had been ever since he met her. Free had stolen her from Twin, who had never spared her of any material possession. Free wanted to be able to give her more than any other man ever could. He wanted to give her the world, and he was ready to make her his wife. There was no questioning the fact that Six loved Free more than anything. She had been loyal to him from the time she laid eyes on him. He couldn't see his life without her, and it was time to make their relationship permanent.

Free stood slowly and followed Big Lou off the aircraft. They made their way through the corridors of the airport as they walked toward the baggage-pickup area.

"Yo, man, you serious about giving this shit up?" Big Lou asked. Big Lou and Free had been pulling capers together since they were young and coming up in Brooklyn. They had quickly made a name for themselves in New York, but after they had robbed Twin, they both skipped town and relocated to Detroit. They tried to stay low-key once they arrived in the Midwest, but they soon discovered that their new city was wide open and prime for the taking. They quickly returned to their old ways, and they reverted to the lifestyle that they knew best. Big Lou and Free were willing to get money by any means necessary as long as the amount of money outweighed the risk.

"Yeah, I'm done. This was my last hit. I've been stacking my paper for a minute now. Me and Six can kick back and just live, you know?" Free said.

"Yo, I don't know anything about that. I ain't gon' never leave this game alone," Big Lou replied.

"I hear you, fam," Free replied as they slapped hands and embraced briefly. "I'ma get at you."

Free and Big Lou grabbed their luggage and went their separate ways. Free located his silver Lexus Coupe and headed home. His hands were moist, and his heart felt as if it would beat out of his chest. Just the thought of settling down made his stomach turn. By marrying Six, he was committing himself to her for life. He was nervous, and he was pushing ninety-five miles per hour on the freeway trying to get to Six. He knew that she would be surprised. He wasn't due back in Detroit for another couple days, but he decided to finish up early and fly back to propose to her. *Is this the chick that I'm supposed to spend the rest of my life with? Is she really down for a nigga, like I'm down for her? Will I be the type of man that she needs me to be?* He knew that the answer to all of his questions was yes. Six was the woman for him. They completed each other, and the closer they became, the more intense his feelings for her became. The potency of his love for her even surprised him. She was his rib, and without her, he couldn't breathe.

As he pulled his luxury vehicle onto his street, he was so nervous that it felt like everything was moving in slow motion. He could see her candy-red, baby-mama Benz gleaming as it sat perfectly in their driveway. *Good, she's here,* he thought as his Lexus slid next to the curb in front of his house.

He reached inside of his jacket pocket and pulled out the box that held the ring inside. He opened it and stared at the flawless cut of the diamond. *It's all or nothing,* he thought as he snapped the box closed and exited the vehicle. He went to the front door, walking slowly as he thought back on his life as a single man. He had always been with Six, but he had enjoyed many chicks on the side over the years.

*Damn, it's time to give all that up. It's time to fly straight,* he thought to himself. Free reached inside his jean pockets in search of his house keys. "Damn, where those mu'fuckas at?" he muttered in frustration as he patted his pockets. He went back to his car to see if he had left the keys inside. He looked everywhere, but his hunt was fruitless.

He jogged back up to the house and rang the doorbell. He could hear the sound of R. Kelly's "12 Play" crooning throughout the house. The music was drowning out the sound of the doorbell as he continued to ring, waiting for Six to answer.

He grew impatient and made his way around the back of the house. He lifted his hand and banged on the back door, knocking hard so Six could hear him. To his surprise, the door cracked slightly. The smell of incense greeted him as soon as he stepped inside the door. All of the curtains were pulled closed, and the only light came from candles that had been strategically placed throughout the house.

"Six!" he yelled as he made his way through the house. He gripped the ring tightly as he rushed to find her. "Baby girl, where you at?" Free received no answer as he walked through the living room. The room was so dark that he lost his balance as he tripped over something that lay in the middle of the floor.

"Damn," he muttered as he reached to the wall and flicked the light switch. His eyes immediately focused on the odd pair of Tims that sat in the middle of his floor. *Fuck, this bitch done had a nigga in my house.*

Free's thoughts went from loving Six to being enraged with her in less than three seconds. He darted up the steps that led to his bedroom and heard moans coming from inside his room. He was squeezing the ring box so tightly that his knuckles hurt from the pressure. He walked to the bedroom door, and his suspicions were confirmed by the sight that he saw. His heart caught in his throat as he watched the love of his life blatantly betraying him. Her moans drowned his eardrums as another man grinded in and out of her, while her eyes rolled in the back of her head.

Free didn't know what happened next. He couldn't control his emotions. All rational thought went out of the window. Red and black filled his vision.

"Bitch, you fucking this nigga? You love this mu'fucka?"

Free was so hurt that darkness clouded his vision.

"You fucking this nigga?" he asked in utter distress as he pulled his pistol from his waistline.

*Pow, pow, pow!*

"Bitch, you fucking this nigga?"

Nothing but darkness and the sounds of the bullets entering flesh could be heard.

*Pow, pow, pow!*

So much red . . . blood flowed freely from the bodies of both victims. Blood on Free's hands . . . blood on his shirt, his shoes, blood in his eyes. The sound of his heart breaking fell on deaf ears. No one was alive to hear him.

*Pow!*

One final bullet. . . .

*Pow!*

*Three Weeks Later*

A pulsating pain shot through Six's body as she slowly opened her eyes. The room was dark, and she was unaware of her surroundings. *Beep, beep, beep, beep.* The steady tone of the machines around her was all that could be heard. The small sound seemed so loud inside her head. Each beep made a sharp explosion go off inside her brain, causing her great pain. Her eyes darted wildly around the room as she searched for something familiar. *Where am I? What happened?* she thought frantically as she tried to move her body. Her lungs felt deprived of air as she struggled to breathe deeply. She wanted to sit up, she wanted to scream for help, but her body would not cooperate. No matter how hard she tried, she was unable to move. Her throat felt like it was on fire, and her heart rate increased dramatically as fear gripped her body. *Beep, beep, beep, beep.* The sound of the machines intensified, and she heard the sound of people rushing into her room.

"Is she all right? What's happening to her?" Six heard Big Lou's voice, and her eyes scanned the many faces that were surrounding her bed as she tried to locate him.

"I'm sorry, sir, you have to wait outside. You can see her once we've stabilized her."

"Is she okay? Just tell me what's happening!" she heard Big Lou demand, his voice frantic with worry.

"Free!" she cried out. His voice was the only voice that she didn't hear. He was the one that she needed right now. *Where is he?*

"I need her calm. Her body is in shock," one of the doctors instructed. Six watched as a young nurse filled a syringe with fluid and injected it into her arm.

"No! Free—I want to see Free!" Six cried in a raspy tone. Her voice was almost inaudible. Her body was weak, but she still fought against the hospital staff as she begged to see her man.

"Look at my hand and count down with me," a doctor stated.

"Five, four, three, two . . ." Before he even got to *one* Six felt her eyelids close involuntarily, taking her to a temporary sanctuary of peace.

Six opened her eyes and immediately sensed the figure who was sitting in the chair beside her bed. She couldn't move her head to see who it was, but she could feel him watching her.

"Free," she whispered, her voice cracking.

"Free's not here, Six. It's me, Big Lou," he whispered as he stood up so that she could see him. "You had me worried for a minute, sis."

"Where is Free? What happened to me? I feel like I can't breathe. Why isn't he here?" she asked.

"You don't remember anything? You don't remember what happened?" Big Lou asked her in bewilderment.

"No, where is he, Lou?"

Before Big Lou could respond, a middle-aged black man entered the room. He was wearing a long lab coat with blue scrubs underneath. Big Lou was grateful for the interruption. He didn't know how to tell Six that Free was dead.

"Six Jones," the doctor stated as he walked up to her bed. He took off his stethoscope and placed the cold metal to her chest. "You are a very lucky young woman."

"What happened to me?" she asked the doctor. The doctor's face immediately expressed confusion as he looked toward Big Lou.

"She doesn't remember," Big Lou answered the doctor's question before he could even ask it.

"Well, Ms. Jones . . ." the doctor started. He was hesitant to inform her of her condition. "You were shot in the head. You are extremely lucky to be alive. That's why you are having such a hard time moving and breathing. During the shooting, a part of your brain called the cerebellum was injured. A part of the brain stem that controls your breathing was also injured. The massive head trauma that you have sustained has caused you to become immobile."

"I'm paralyzed?" Six whispered with tears in her eyes. She stared up toward the ceiling as she tried to process what the doctor was telling her.

"Not exactly. The damage is not permanent. But your body has to learn how to function again. That's why you are hooked up to the breathing machine. Your brain is not sending the correct signals to the rest of your body. You can't breathe or move on your own yet."

"Where is Free? I need him," she said as her tears began to flow. She gasped for air, struggling to breathe.

"She doesn't know?" the doctor asked as he looked toward Big Lou again.

"I can't tell her, yo," Big Lou said as he gripped Six's hand and tears began to well in his own eyes.

"Tell me what?" she asked. "Where is he? Big Lou, where is Free?"

The doctor excused himself so that he could give them some privacy.

"Six, he's gone. He shot you; then he turned the gun on himself."

Six didn't respond. She stared at Big Lou as tears streamed endlessly down her face. *He can't be gone. He told me he would never leave me. Why would he do this to me? Free, I need you.* Her body shuddered as she thought about the death of Free. He had been her best friend and

her heart. She couldn't find any words to describe how she felt; her heart was numb.

She closed her eyes, and images of Free entered her mind. The entire scene instantly came
back to her as she played it back in her head. She
could hear the blast from the gun in her ears.
She could feel his pain as he asked her repeatedly, *Do you love this nigga? Do you love this
nigga?* Six saw the spark from the barrel of the
gun as Free pulled the trigger. "Oh my God! Big
Lou! Oh God! He can't be gone. I can't do this
without him. I need him," she cried. Tears of despair stained her cheeks as she lay helplessly in
the hospital bed. "How did this happen? Where
is he? Big Lou—"

"He's gone, Six . . . he's gone," Big Lou said as
he held her hand.

"I just want to be alone," she stated as she
closed her eyes.

Big Lou nodded slowly. "All right. I'll be right
outside if you need me."

"Big Lou . . . when is his funeral?" Six asked
before he stepped out.

"You've been in a coma for the past three weeks.
The funeral was two weeks ago." He waited for her
to reply, but when she didn't, he walked out of the
room.

She couldn't stop the tears from escaping from her eyes. She was deeply hurt by Free's death. Her soul ached unbearably as she tried to imagine her life without him in it. *How did we get here? How did I let this happen?* Six stared at the ceiling as she thought about when her life began to spiral out of control.

# Chapter One

*One Year Earlier*

Six stood beside the Audi S8 and tapped her foot anxiously as she waited for Free to exit the prison gates.

"You nervous?" Big Lou asked. She had been silent the entire trip there, and she seemed to be lost in her own thoughts. She silently hoped that her man would be the same as he was before he went in. She knew that the life and times of an inmate were hard and hoped that time hadn't changed him too much.

"Nah, I'm cool," she replied. Just as the words came from her mouth, the clanging of the large metal gates could be heard and Free came waltzing out. He turned around and stuck his middle fingers up at the guards who were positioned in the towers above each gate and then held his arms open for Six, who was running toward him full speed.

"Oh my God, baby, I missed you so much," she cried as she jumped into his arms and wrapped her arms tightly around his neck. He spun her around wildly and lifted her off the ground.

"Let me look at you," he said eagerly as he placed her on her feet and held up her hand as he twirled her around.

Six blushed as she felt Free's eyes roam her body. Big Lou approached the couple and embraced his friend.

"Big Lou!" Free exclaimed as he hugged his closest friend.

"Nigga, I see they were feeding your ass in there," Big Lou clowned as he noticed Free's change in appearance. Free had gained thirty or so pounds of muscle from eating the prison food and the everyday weight-lifting routine he had picked up while in prison.

"Shut up, Lou, my baby look good," Six defended playfully as she walked ahead of them to the car. When she was out of ear's reach Free turned to Big Lou.

"Yo, man how she been acting while I was away?" Free asked out of concern. He wanted to know what had been going on with her for the past three years. He had not expected her to wait for him and was pleasantly surprised that she had.

"Man, Six is the same chick she was when you left. She held you down. I never heard about her entertaining no other niggas. As far as I know, she was faithful. I know she been kind of hurting financially though. I been helping out when I can, but shit has changed, and times are rough, feel me?"

Free slapped hands with Big Lou and replied, "Yeah, I feel you. Thanks for watching out for her."

*Beep, beep!*

"Let's get out of here, baby," Six yelled from the car as she honked the horn lightly.

When Free got into the car Six pulled a shopping bag from the backseat. "Go ahead and get fresh, baby. That jail suit got to go."

Six drove home while Free and Big Lou let the road lull them to sleep. She looked over at her man who was sitting in the passenger seat and a tear fell from her eyes. She was so happy that he was finally home with her. The past three years had been one constant struggle. Emotionally and financially she was spent. The lawyers for Free's trial had taken most of their money, and she had been struggling to make her ends meet and maintain her high-class lifestyle. Things had gotten so bad that she had even began working as a bartender in a local strip joint called the Kitty

Kat. She knew that Free wouldn't like it, but she did what she had to do to maintain. They pulled up to her one-bedroom apartment, and she announced, "We're here, wake up."

Free drowsily looked up at the worn apartment building and then over at Six. "How long you been staying here?"

"About two years now," she replied. "I couldn't afford the condo," she stated, referring to the luxury high-rise condominium that she and Free had shared before his arrest.

Six exited the car, and Free looked toward the backseat and said, "Big Lou, I'll be right back. Let me get her settled." He got out of the car and put his hand on the small of Six's back as he followed her up to her apartment.

"What are we going to do?" Six asked Free. She was dead broke, and now that Free was home, she needed him to take care of her like he had always done.

"We gon' get money like we always have. You don't have to worry about anything, Six. I'm home now," he said as he caressed her hair.

"I know, but you don't know how hard it's been for me. I'm living in this fucking hellhole. I am struggling to pay the rent, and my bills are piled up to the ceiling!"

"What happened to the money we had stacked up before I went in?" Free asked.

"Your lawyers are what happened, Free," Six replied.

"How much we got left?"

"We ain't got shit left. It's about two thousand dollars in my account," Six whined.

"Two stacks! You blew through a hundred Gs in three years?" Free questioned.

"Why are you yelling at me? I told you your lawyers were expensive."

"I'm not yelling at you, ma. I'm just trying to understand why you hurting so bad. You ain't working? You couldn't get a gig?"

Six crossed her arms and replied, "Of course I got a job, Free. I wasn't just sitting back spending your dough. I'm working at the strip club, but that only goes so far."

Free's eyes widened in disapproval. "The club? You been shaking your ass for dollars while I've been locked up, showing all these niggas what belong to me?" he asked angrily.

"I'm bartending, Free, so calm down! What else was I supposed to do? I needed money, so Sparkle hooked me up with the bartending thing. Don't make it a bigger deal than what it is," Six defended, her voice raised a bit out of frustration.

"Damn, Six! I just got out of the joint today, and you already in my ear about some cash. Let me get my head together first. I never knew you to be the type to gold dig."

"Gold dig?" Six exclaimed. Her hands shot to her hips, and she scrunched her face in confusion. "Free, whatever! Your ass has been behind bars for the past three years, and not once have I thought of stepping out on you. I had the opportunity to say *fuck you* and move on to the next nigga, but I didn't. Yeah, I'm trying to find out what's up on some money. I'm broke. Niggas is knocking down my door asking for the rent . . . The world didn't stop when you went away. I still had to survive out here on my own."

Free turned his back to her and headed toward the door.

"Where are you going?" she yelled.

"To the block," he replied shortly. He was obviously steamed and wanted to get out of Six's presence before the small argument escalated. That's how they were . . . hot and cold . . . on and off . . . love and hate . . . their relationship wasn't one that had been pulled out of the pages of a fairy tale, but at the end of the day, all they had was one another. Despite the petty fights their love ran deep.

"You just got home. Your boys on the block are more important than me?"

*Here she goes with that shit,* Free thought to himself. Without answering, he left the house to clear his head. He was well aware that he needed to get on his grind. He still had an unsettled debt to pay, but the last thing he needed was Six stressing him out more by bitching over cash that he didn't have. He knew that she was high maintenance, but she would have to be patient until he came up with a hustle plan that would make him rich but wouldn't send him back to prison.

"You good?" Big Lou asked as Free got back into the car.

"Yeah, I'm good," he replied as he pulled away from the curb.

The liberated feeling that Free felt as he maneuvered his way through the city streets was better than anything that he had felt in a long time. The subwoofers in the car were on point as the two men pulled up onto Big Lou's block.

Big Lou and Free exited the vehicle to approach Big Lou's house. A familiar face called out to Lou.

"Big Lou! Hold up a minute, man," a voice yelled from up the street.

Free noticed a familiar face jog up the block toward them. Ronnie was the local weed man in Detroit. He got his supply from Big Lou, who had a crazy weed connect out of New York.

"Look at this mu'fucka," Big Lou whispered to Free. Ronnie's pants hung below his waist, and it was obvious that he was still wearing yesterday's drawers. The dingy color of the supposed-to-be white fabric and the dirt underneath his fingernails symbolized exactly how dirty the nigga was. His yellow gap-toothed smile and balled-up Force Ones were a dead giveaway to his grimy tactics. He kept looking behind him and from side to side as he approached. "This bum-ass nigga," Big Lou mumbled as he shifted his stance. "What up, Ronnie?"

"Yo, Big Lou, I need to holla at you about something, man," Ronnie replied as he continued to look from side to side.

"What up, fam? Time is money, nigga—talk," Big Lou stated.

Ronnie eyed Free suspiciously and then said, "Can we step inside or something? This a private matter, you know?"

"Nigga, you know Free. What's good?"

"No disrespect, Free. I just need to holla at Big Lou on some private shit, you know. I mean, I heard about your beef with them Russians, and I'm not trying to be associated in that shit, you feel me?"

Free looked at Ronnie with a calm expression on his face and stated, "I don't know what you talking about. Handle your business though, bruh."

"Nigga, get the fuck out of here with all that privacy bullshit. Get at me when you ready to talk," Big Lou stated harshly as he and Free stepped up the sidewalk and sat down on the porch.

"What is up with your people?" Free asked as he made himself comfortable on Big Lou's porch, positioning himself so that he could see the entire length of the city block.

"Man, I ain't want to be all in your business, but word is out about you and that Russian cat. Niggas gon' be scared to fuck with you for a while. Word is you owe that mu'fucka like a mill or something."

"Niggas talk too much about shit they don't know, nah, mean," Free stated with apparent anger in his voice.

"What really happened? What did you do that got those Russians gunning for your head?"

"You remember the day I got locked up?" Free asked.

"Yeah, you was driving up to New York, but got pulled over by a cop. I never understood why you took them mu'fuckas on a high-speed chase. You was playing with them pigs," Big Lou stated with laughter in his voice. "Those crackers chased your ass all the way up Interstate 75."

"I didn't have a choice. I had fifteen keys in the car with me," Free admitted. He had never told anyone the true story of what had happened that day.

"And you only did three years? Free, you snitching?" Big Lou asked, knowing that the excessive amount of cocaine that Free had was enough to have gotten him a life sentence.

"Hell, nah. Come on, fam, you know me better than that. They ain't catch me with the bricks, just the pistol I had. I shook the police so I could get rid of the product. I tossed that shit. That type of weight would've put me under the jail. I didn't have a choice."

"What does all this have to do with the Russians?"

"It was their weight. Claude is out of a hundred and fifty thousand dollars."

"Damn! A hundred fifty?" Big Lou asked in disbelief.

"A hundred fifty," Free confirmed. "I just got out, and I know he's waiting to hear from me. I got to have something to offer when I call him, though. He gon' be trying to speak money, and that's something I don't have right now. Six is stressing over money, and I got this shit on my mind."

"Yo, you know I got you, fam. Whatever you need . . . well, not whatever, nigga. I ain't got a hundred fifty, but whatever else you need, I'm with you."

"Good looking out," Free said. "What I really need to know is how much the bricks going for?"

Free sat back on his best friend's porch and watched as Big Lou's block made money. Free could tell that a lot had changed since his reign had ended. The entire operation looked sloppy. Whoever was running things hadn't trained his people well enough. *These niggas is making transactions on street corners, and they keeping the work on 'em. Don't nobody stand on corners no more,* Free thought, disgusted at how off their hustle was.

"This cat named Brick got the joints for twenty-five a pop."

"Damn, a quarter a key," Free replied in disbelief. He had never paid more than 16.5 per kilo, and he didn't intend on starting now. He came to the conclusion that Brick was definitely overcharging. "He's taxing niggas like that?"

"Man, Brick the only one in the city that got 'em. There was a drought on the streets after you got hit. You know them Russians weren't fucking with none of us, so nobody could get their hands on work. Brick came through a couple months into your bid and took over. He had them for sale, and even though his shit ain't as good as the

Russians, it was all we had to choose from. He knows he's the only one in town with the weight so he charges whatever he wants." Big Lou sat back in the white porch chair and smiled at Free. "You trying to get back on?"

Free shook his head and replied, "Hell, no, you know I ain't working underneath nobody, and I'm not paying no outrageous prices for the work either. I'll find another connect."

"Well, you might have a hard time getting anything off in Detroit. That nigga Britain is nutty as hell. If you ain't down with him, you ain't eating. He got all these niggas around here shook. The only niggas that's really getting money like that is Brick and his people. He's spoon-feeding everybody else."

"Fuck Brick. Ain't no man gon' stop me from eating, nah, mean?" Free asked as he thought about how badly he needed to come up. Just as the words came out his mouth, a caravan of expensive cars came rolling down Big Lou's block. Benzes, Lexuses, and Escalades rolled slowly down the street. Loud music was coming out of the custom speakers of each vehicle, and each car was sitting on its own set of twenty-two inch rims. The windows of the cars were rolled up, and the faces of the men that sat inside were hidden by the dark tint.

"What is that all about?" Free inquired, nodding in the direction of the cars.

"That's Brick's young goon squad. Those are the only people that he keeps close to him. They ride around once a day to make their presence known."

Free knew that they were trying to stunt. They were riding high, and they wanted everybody in the city to know it. Once again, Free shook his head. Brick was running a drug ring that was destined to get him and his crew put in a federal prison. They had two qualities that were bound to get you locked up. They were flashy and stupid. Niggas riding around in one-hundred-thousand-dollar cars did nothing but draw attention to the already hot block where hustlers stood on corners alternating crack sales. *A couple years back, I would have stuck those flashy niggas up,* he thought to himself.

"You fucking with him?" Free asked.

Big Lou stood up and opened the screen door to the house. "Hell, nah. That drug shit is dead right now. A nigga like me values his freedom. You ain't seen the news?"

Free shook his head and then got up to follow Big Lou into the house.

"This shit has been all over the TV for weeks now. Brick got into some shit. One of his workers got nabbed a couple months ago. Dumb mu'fucka gon' try to venture out and do some side hustling. The nigga ended up selling to an undercover narc."

"Damn," Free commented.

"You ain't heard the most of it . . . Watch this shit," Big Lou said as he turned on his forty-inch plasma. CNNs Nancy Grace appeared on the screen, and her voice filled the room.

"According to federal prosecutor Brant Stallworth, the government has a witness that can give in-depth testimonies regarding Britain Adams's involvement in an international drug ring. Britain Adams has a street alias of 'Brick,' and he has a loyal following of young men who have terrorized the city of Detroit. Allegedly, since his position as kingpin three years ago, the violent crime rate has skyrocketed in the area. He is charged with several counts of murder, distribution of a controlled substance, and extortion. If convicted, Britain Adams will be facing a life sentence in a federal penitentiary."

Big Lou turned off the television and shook his head in contempt. "The worst part about it is that the key witness is one of the cats he kept in his inner circle, so he knows everything. I'm talking names of the connect, stash spots, where bodies lie . . . the whole nine."

"Sound like your man Brick don't know who's who in his own camp," Free stated. *This nigga Brick set himself up. You always supposed to know who you got in your circle,* he thought.

"Word on the street is he got a fed in his pocket that can tell him where they holding the witness. Only thing is he can't do anything about it. They got the scope on him tough. The nigga can't take a shit without the feds knowing about it."

"Sound like his days are numbered," Free said as he shook his head from side to side.

"Looks that way, don't it?" Big Lou agreed.

For the first time Free realized that the drug game was dried up. The clientele was there, but Brick had made it too hot for anybody to do anything. He looked at Big Lou and then said, "I'ma get at you later, fam."

They slapped hands, and Free prepared to leave. Before he walked out of the door, Big Lou called out to him.

"Yo, Free!"

Free stopped walking and turned to face his friend.

"Let me know if you need me."

"Thanks, man, I'ma get at you."

Nighttime had fallen quickly, and Free was mentally exhausted from trying to come up with some type of plan. He was riding through the city streets when he noticed the flashing red and blue lights behind him. He pulled over to the side of the road and placed his hands on the steering wheel. He didn't want to give the cop any reason to jump stupid, so he waited patiently as he approached the window.

"Alfree Woodard," the officer announced smugly. Free already knew who it was. He recognized his voice. It was the same detective who had locked him up three years ago. He had some type of personal vendetta against Free.

"Detective Wade," Free acknowledged as he nodded, still keeping his hands on the wheel. He knew that Wade wouldn't have a problem putting a bullet in him, so he made sure that he didn't make the wrong move.

"It's kind of late for you to be out here, ain't it?"

"Just running to the store for my girl," Free replied. The detective laughed slightly and repeated, "Running to the store for your girl." His demeanor turned hostile as he continued. "Cut the bullshit, Free. I'm watching you. I'm here waiting for the opportunity to send you back to prison." With those words Detective Lonnie Wade walked back to his unmarked squad car and drove off, winking at Free before he was out of sight.

"Fuck!" Free yelled out as he hit the dashboard. He knew that the detective's eyes would be on him for awhile. If he made any type of attempt to reenter the drug game, the detective would send him back to prison, and this time it would be for the long haul. *How am I going to come up with this money?*


Six felt guilty about the argument that she had started with Free. She knew that he was a good man. He had always treated her with respect and showered her with material possessions. *Damn, I shouldn't have gone off like I did. I know if he's got it, I've got it. I got to stick by his side right now and let him know that I'm here.*

Six was consumed by her thoughts as she prepared a romantic atmosphere for her man to come home to. She was so used to him spoiling her, and now that he couldn't, she was upset. She knew that she was going to have to let Free know that she was there through whatever. He had carried her for so long and only stopped because he had been arrested. She knew that it was her turn to be strong for her man, and that is exactly what she planned to do from that point on. She looked at the clock that read 4:30 A.M. and felt her heart sink. She didn't even know if Free planned to come home. The empty knot in the bottom of her stomach had her sick with uncertainty. He had never stayed out all night before, but they both had said things that should have never been spoken, and she knew that he was feeling the exact same way that she was . . . guilty. She lit every candle in the house and turned out the lights, creating a romantic ambiance in the tiny apartment. Then she showered and slipped into a black Victoria's Secret camisole and matching thong. Turning on the song that she and Free fell asleep to every night, Six sat back and listened as Biggie kicked his lyrics to "Me & My Bitch."

*But you was my bitch, the one who'd never snitch*

*Love me when I'm broke or when I'm filthy fuckin' rich*

Six's eyes watched the clock and as each minute passed a little bit of her heart broke even more. Free was her best friend, and she needed him to know that she was down for him. She knew that Free wasn't the type of man who would be down for long. He would pick up the broken pieces; she would just have to give him time. She was stressed and had blown up out of frustration, but in the back of her mind, she knew that he would take care of her. She balled up on the couch and stared at the front door. *I hope he comes home.*

As if her thoughts had summoned him the locks clicked on the front door, and Free walked in. He stared at Six as she lay on the couch, and she returned his gaze. They both could sense the other's remorse, but they didn't feel that it was necessary to speak any words. They knew each other like the backs of their own hand and already knew what the other was thinking.

He sighed and walked over to her, he lifted her head and sat down. She rested her head in his lap as he stroked her hair and inhaled the scent of her Love Spell body spray. His touch was so gentle that he sent shivers up her spine. Six was so glad that Free had come home. Everything that she had planned on saying was easily forgotten. She just felt good being in his presence.

"I'm sorry," she whispered. "I understand what you're going through, baby, and I am here for you. We're together for life, and when you are down, I am here to help pick you up. You take care of me, Free; you always have, and I know you always will. I was just aggravated with everything. It was hard for me while you were away. I put pressure on you when it wasn't necessary. I love you, Free, and I'm here with you. I know it's only a matter of time before we're on top again, but I want you to know that I'm with you even when we're on the bottom."

Free sat back and listened as Six talked. He knew the type of chick who he had on his team. Free understood why Six was worried, but he was a man, and he was going to make their ends meet by any means necessary. She was his queen, and he had spoiled her so much that she had become accustomed to living the life. He was determined to provide her with that lifestyle again. He knew that until he could do that she would stick by his side.

Looking down at Six as her head rested in his lap, all of his tensions melted away. Just being near her again felt good. Everything about the two of them was always so right . . . so on point as if their existence had been synchronized to the same clock. He looked at her voluptuous figure and felt the swell of his dick rise against his jeans.

Six sat up and straddled Free, grinding her hips against his concealed manhood. She kissed him seductively, exploring his mouth with her tongue. Her body moved to the rhythm of the song, and Free's hands gripped her ample behind, his fingertips leaving dents in her soft skin as her breasts pressed against his chest. Free grabbed Six's backside firmly and looked down at the thong that had disappeared between the crack of her ass. He picked her up with her legs still wrapped around him and carried her into the bedroom.

Her fat lips were a beautiful sight to Free. He had gone his entire stretch in prison without feeling the inside of a woman, and her engorged clitoris made his mouth water in anticipation. He licked his lips as he placed a finger to Six's opening. She sucked his long finger inside of her, using her vaginal muscles to entice her man.

Free closed his eyes as he felt her walls tighten around his finger. Six was soaked in her own juices, and she couldn't wait for her man to please her. She held onto him tightly as he gently placed her on the bed and pulled off the tiny thong. Six sat up, reached for his belt buckle, and removed Free's jeans. His thick eight inches stood at attention in her face, and she couldn't help but to taste him. She devoured him into her mouth, making him disappear and reappear over and over. Free placed his hands on her head and gently guided her as she sucked him like a lollipop, her tongue stroking the vein on the back of his shaft.

Six's head game was superb and it was designed just for him. Her full lips, deep throat, and slick tongue were all trained personally by Free, and all she wanted to do was please him. She ran her tongue up and down his length and kissed the tip gently, causing his toes to curl.

Free pushed Six back onto the bed, and they positioned themselves into the sixty-nine position. He opened her lips with his tongue and tasted her wetness as he gently ravaged her womanly pearl. His tongue flicked back and forth, fast and then slow . . . firm and then soft.

"Aggh," she moaned as she rotated her hips, making love to Free's mouth. The better he made her feel, the better she sucked his dick. She couldn't help it, he was making her go crazy, and she wanted to please him until he exploded. She wanted him to release all of the built-up tension from years of lockup.

Moans couldn't help but to escape her lips as he tickled her insides with his fingers and caressed her clit with his tongue. She was riding his face like a cowboy and moving her head up and down like she was bobbing for apples. Free was large, and she wanted him inside of her, but she was feeling too good to stop him. He ate her out, and she hit him off until they both reached their climax. She swallowed his seed leaving his manhood spotless, and her back arched with the grace of a ballerina as she came in his mouth. They both had reached ecstasy and in the process released all of their built-up anxiety.

Makeup sex was the best between Six and Free. It was so good that sometimes they looked forward to fighting just so they could make up all over again. Too exhausted to get up and do anything, Six wrapped herself in Free's arms.

"I'ma take care of you. You deserve the best, and that's what I'm gon' give you. That's my word."

"I already have the best. The world is ours, Free."

Free had to smile at her words because he knew that she was the perfect woman for him and that she would always hold him down.

"The world is ours, ma."

With those words, they drifted into a comfortable sleep.

# Chapter Two

It seemed like the morning came too quickly because Six was still groggy and exhausted from the night before. She felt the covers being lifted off her and frowned as the draft of cold morning air caused goose bumps to form on her skin. She knew that Free wanted to pick up where they had left off, but she was too tired.

"Baby stop . . ." she mumbled as she felt him run his finger down her thigh. "Free, your hands are cold . . . stop," she whined as she kept her eyes closed, not wanting to awaken fully. It wasn't until she heard the shower running did Six realize something wasn't right. The sound of running water sparked confusion in her mind.

"Six! Bring me some soap out of the closet!" she heard Free yell. The hands that were touching her body suddenly felt like tiny knives scratching her skin as she realized that they didn't belong to Free. She sat up instantly to find three white men standing in the room, one of whom was standing over her tracing the outline of her ass with a black .38.

"Fre—" Six tried to yell out to Free, but before she could even get his name out of her mouth, a sweaty hand covered it, silencing her, and three pistols were aimed in her direction, the .38-caliber pistol pointed directly at her temple.

"Shut up, bitch," one of them calmly instructed.

Six's heart felt like it had sunk into her stomach, and fear filled her body. In any other situation she would have known how to react. She would have taken her chances and reached for the nightstand where her .22 pistol was kept. She would have warned Free that someone was in the house. She would have done something, but this situation was different. She had been caught off guard, and the man that had the steel pressed to the side of her head intimidated her. There was something about the way that he looked at her that told her he wouldn't hesitate to pull the trigger. For the first time in a long time she was afraid. She didn't know what was going to happen or even why they had come.

The men's eyes ogled her body, and she wanted to pull up the covers, but was frozen in place. Everyone in the room heard the running water stop. The men cocked their weapons, and Six's body stiffened when she heard the hammer to the .38-caliber pistol pull back. Six did the only thing that she could do and lifted her eyes to the sky and prayed silently. *Please God, don't let them kill Free . . . please don't let him come into this room.* Six wasn't even worried about her well-being. The only thing that she could think of was Free. She didn't know what she would do if something happened to him.

Free wrapped a towel around his waist and then made his way into the bedroom. He opened the door and the sight of a gun threatening Six's existence enraged him. He ran toward the bed, but was halted by a tall white man who aimed a .357 Ruger in his direction.

"Free!" Six yelled out, afraid that he would be shot. Her heart was beating like a drum and tears began to swell in her eyes.

Free's mind was focused on getting to her; he wasn't thinking about the hole that the Ruger would leave through his chest if fired. He grabbed the wrist of the man and punched him hard in the face causing blood to flood from his nose.

*"Aghh, fuck!"* The man yelled out in pain as he cupped his face with both hands and dropped to his knees in excruciation. In one swift movement, Free snatched the weapon from his hands

and pointed it toward the bed where the infamous Claude Jean, member of the Russian mafia, stood next to a terrified Six. Free was working straight off of emotion and didn't notice the third Russian intruder until he had his gun pressed against Six's head. Claude laughed as he jabbed his gun into her skin.

"Free, what the fuck are you doing? What are you, Superman now?" He continued to chuckle and then firmly stated, "Don't be stupid. Put the gun down." Free hesitated as he looked at Six, who had closed her eyes.

"What are you going to do?" Claude continued, "Are you going to kill me, Free? Before you even pull the trigger, her brains will be all over the bedspread." Free dropped the gun and glared at Claude, who now had the gun on Six's bare breasts, the cold steel making her dark nipples stand at attention and enraging Free even more. Free could see Six trembling, and his jaw clenched as he gritted his teeth.

"What is a woman so beautiful doing with a man like Free?" Claude asked as he continued to fondle Six's nipples with the gun. She slapped his hand away, and he chuckled. "Someone like you could be living lavishly. If you play your cards right, I might make you my mistress," Claude said as he lusted after Six's naked frame. He pulled back the covers so that he could see her entire body.

"Don't touch me," Six spoke through clenched teeth in a frightened tone as she roughly snatched the covers to cover herself.

"You black bitches have no manners. Your men don't know how to train you. I was trying to offer you something more than Free could ever give you, but your eyes tell me you have chosen Free. So fuck it. You're his whore, so his debt just became your debt too."

Free was infuriated at the disrespect, but he knew that Claude would not hesitate to kill Six, so he kept his cool.

"She must be the reason why you forgot to contact me and let me know you were released from prison."

"If you touch her—"

"Yeah, yeah, yeah . . . Let's skip the dramatics, Free. You know how I work. If I wanted to kill the bitch, she'd already be dead. I came here to talk about my money."

Free remained silent and stared at Six as she stared frightfully back at him.

"You take fifteen kilos of my good, pure, Russian cocaine on consignment, and then you get busted with them. That's $150,000 worth of product I'm out of. Then you get out of prison and don't even contact me to make arrangements. That bothers me, Free. . . . I shouldn't have to come here looking for you."

"I've only been out a couple hours, Claude. I'll have the money. . . . You know I'm good for it," Free stated defiantly, the apparent anger showing in his voice.

"You used to be good for it! That's the only reason why you are still breathing. You served your time like a man, and not once did you mention my family's name. I respect you for that, but I won't commend you for it. That is what you were supposed to do. We want our money, Free. $150,000 plus interest."

"How much?" Free asked.

"$250,000 . . . a quarter million. You have six months. If you don't come up with my money by then, I will murder everybody that you have ever loved, beginning with her."

The Russians walked out of the room, but before Claude exited the apartment he yelled out, "I will be back in six months."

As soon as they heard the door close, Free rushed to Six's side as she broke down in his arms. She buried her head in his shoulders, and her body shook uncontrollably as Free rocked back and forth trying to console her. It was the first time that he had ever seen Six so weak, and it hurt him deeply. He didn't say anything, he just held onto her. He loved her more than he loved himself, and he was determined to keep her safe. He would not let Claude touch her again . . . Free would be prepared next time, and the consequences would be death.

"Shh, it's all right. . . . You're safe now," Free comforted her.

"What are we gonna do, Free?" Six asked as the tears flowed down her face. Six was afraid, not only for herself but for Free. She couldn't live without him by her side, and she was afraid of what was going to happen next.

"Don't worry about none of this. I'm gon' handle it," Free said reassuringly as a thousand thoughts raced through his mind.

"Let's just leave. . . . We can leave Detroit tonight," Six pleaded. She could see the look on Free's face, and she knew that running from the Russians was not an option. "Free, please. Let's just pick up and go. . . . We can go as far away from here as we can. They will never find us. Just say you'll leave with me."

As much as Free wanted to give Six her way, he couldn't, not in this circumstance. "Nah, I owe them those bricks. I'm a man, and I'm gonna pay my debt, but for them touching you, they gon' die. That's my word." Free watched as Six nodded her head. He felt guilty about dragging her into his business with the Russians. It had nothing to do with her, but he knew that she was his weakness. The Russians would use her against him, and he was determined to get her out of it.

For the rest of the day, Six and Free stayed away from each other. They were both consumed by their own thoughts. Free knew that his situation was crucial. He needed money like he needed air in his lungs, and if he didn't come up with a resolution soon, the Russians would shatter his world. Not only did he need to grind to please Six, he needed to grind to save her life. He knew that Claude would make good on his threat, and Free would die before he let anything happen to her.

Six had so much on her mind she couldn't think straight. Free was in trouble, and no matter how much he tried to downplay the situation, she knew that it was serious. It was a matter of life and death. Six sat in the middle of their bed with her legs crossed and the monthly bills sitting in front of her. It seemed like her life had been turned upside down, and the only thing that could fix her problems was money. Rent was due tomorrow, and they didn't have enough to cover everything. Six didn't know what to do. She knew that Free's mind was occupied with thoughts of Claude, and she didn't want to bother him with anything else.

It was crazy how quickly her life had changed. Before Free had been sent to prison, she had everything she could ever want, and there were never any arguments or worries over funds. Now that was all that seemed to matter. How they were going to pay off their debts? Whether it was Claude, bill collectors, or the landlord . . . they all wanted their money. Six got up and walked into the living room where Free was sitting in deep contemplation.

"I'ma hit the block for a minute," he said as he stood and wrapped his arms around Six's waist.

"Okay," she replied absentmindedly. She knew that he was going to handle some business. She had some business to tend to of her own, and this would give her the opportunity to take care of it. "I think I might go see my dad," Six said, knowing that he would help her with the bills and be able to calm her soul about the money issues.

Six's father had been helping her cover her rent since Free had first gone to jail. No matter how long or hard she worked, her pockets always came up short, and she always had to go to her daddy to help pay the extra. Ben Jones didn't mind, though. Free had helped him out plenty of times before he went in for his three-year stretch. Free always made sure Jones's pockets were right, and he always took good care of his only daughter, so Jones felt obligated to return the favor. Six was close to her father. Before Free, he was the only person who ever cared about her, and she knew that he would always help her if he could. She knocked on his door lightly and waited anxiously for him to answer.

"Hey, Daddy," she said when he opened the door. She tried to put on her best smile and sound as normal as possible, but her father knew her too well. He could see right through her.

"Hey, baby girl," he greeted as he opened the door for her and led her inside. Her father lived in a small house in a modest neighborhood on the outskirts of the city. "I hear Free's out."

"Yeah, he's home. Three years is a long time. I'm just glad that we're together again," Six explained with worried eyes.

Jones sensed his daughter's disposition and asked, "If you're so happy, why are you sitting here all frowned up, looking like you are carrying the weight of the world on your shoulders?"

Six shrugged her shoulders and responded, "Things are just real tight right now, Daddy. You know I was barely making it while Free was locked up. I guess I never thought about what we would do when he got out. I just assumed that things would go back to how they were before." Six watched as her daddy pulled out a bag of weed and rolled up a joint. He was an OG and gave the best advice when he was high.

"Six, part of the reason why I gave Free my blessing regarding you is because I knew that he would do anything to give you the world. I knew that he would take care of you, and he has. He just finished doing a bid, so it's gon' take him a minute to get back on his feet. Until then, you have to hold him down. You know that I'm gon' help you in any way that I can, and Free don't have to know about that. He's a real man, and you belong to him now. He ain't gon' want no other man taking care of his home. . . . It don't matter that I'm your daddy. So this can be our secret."

Jones reached in his pocket and handed Six two thousand dollars, enough to pay her rent, and then continued. "I know Free had quite a bit of change saved up, but he paid that price for his freedom. Those damn lawyers will do that to you. The important thing is that he's out. You don't know what it's like being a young black man with a record, baby girl. Your daddy knows about that, so I can relate to what Free is going through. Don't sweat him. . . . Just ride with him. Let him get used to breathing this free air again. Once he gets used to being home, everything will fall into place." He stopped talking to puff on the joint while Six sat in his old La-Z-Boy, absorbing her father's words.

"Is that all that's bothering you?" Jones asked his daughter, noticing her contemplation.

Six nodded her head and replied, "Yeah, Daddy, that's it. I'm good; I just got a lot on my mind." Six had decided on the way there not to tell her father about their run-in with the Russians. She didn't want him worrying, and she also didn't want her father confronting the Russians. She knew that he didn't care how big or dangerous Claude's operation was—her father would kill them or die in the process for laying hands on his little girl. In his day, he was a notorious murder for hire and would put in work if he had to. *No, it's better if I keep that to myself,* she thought as she rose from her seat and hugged her father.

"I love you, Daddy. Thanks for everything."

"I love you too, baby girl," he said in between tokes. "Tell Free to come see me. He's been out for a couple days now, and he ain't come to holla at your old man. I need to talk to him about something."

"I will," Six replied as she walked toward the door.

"Six!" Jones called out.

"Yeah, Daddy?" she said as she turned around to face him.

"Word on the street is Free owes the Russians a lot of money. You need to be careful," he warned her.

"You know how niggas talk in the streets, Daddy. Everybody spreading rumors. Free is good," Six replied quickly. She didn't realize that he already knew about Free's beef with the Russians. For him to know about it meant that it was traveling down the hood grapevine and she knew that couldn't be a good thing.

"Yeah, I hear you holding your man down, not wanting to put his business out. I already know the deal so there ain't no need to lie to me. Those Russian mu'fuckas ain't nothing to play with."

"I hear you, Daddy."

"I'm serious, Six. Be careful. The best way to get to a man is through his woman. Always remember that. Do you still have the pistol I bought you for your eighteenth birthday?"

Six lifted her pants leg and revealed the tiny .22 pistol that was strapped to her ankle in a holster.

"That's my girl. Make sure Free comes to see me and soon."

He kissed Six on her forehead and she walked out the door. Just as she stepped off of his porch she saw a pearl-white Rolls-Royce pull up in front of her father's house. *Who is driving a Royce through the hood?* She asked herself as she made her way to her car. A dark-skinned dude with a five o'clock shadow stepped out of the vehicle. He was clean in a white linen button-down and matching baggy linen shorts. Six silently wondered what the guy was doing there to see her father. She could feel his eyes watching her from behind the designer shades he wore and she turned her head to avoid his gaze as she passed him. He nodded a hello at her as he stepped to the side to watch her walk by, but she disregarded him without acknowledgement. She was too busy thinking about her father's warning regarding the Russians.

Her father's words kept playing in her head and Six was grateful for his wisdom. He was always there when she needed him and he always made her feel better when she had a problem. The simple fact that he had warned her about the Russians told her that they were dangerous and made her think about their intrusion that morning. *If we can pay off the Russians, everything will be okay.*

Six began plotting ways for them to come up. She knew that they needed a hustle, she just didn't know what it would be. It was clear that Free couldn't enter the dope game. There was too big of a risk associated with it. Free would need to move some serious weight in order to achieve that goal. *The dope game is out. I can't see my baby get locked up again, so we definitely not fucking with that. We're in this together. I know Free is gon' try to carry this by himself, but I'm not taking no for an answer. We have to get this money.*

# Chapter Three

Six sent the rent and bills off as soon as she made it home, but the stress of needing money still worried her. *What happens if we don't come up with the Russians' money?* she pondered as she paced back and forth in the tiny living room. She didn't even want to think about what the Russians would do to her if Free didn't pay up. Her father's words from earlier that day kept replaying in her mind. "The best way to get to a man is through his woman." The phrase echoed over and over, and it was beginning to make a small headache form behind her temples.

Ever since he had said that to her, Six had been plotting different ways she could use the warning to her advantage. She worked at the Kitty Kat, the most popular strip joint in town. It was where all the ballers and get-money cats in Detroit went to relax. She had seen so much game run on men in that club that she was sure that the answer to their problems could be found

within those walls. So much money came in
and out of the club and the dancers were always
scheming in order to get paid. Six knew that
she could never stoop so low for money, but she
knew somebody who would . . . her best friend,
Sparkle.

Sparkle had hustled plenty of men out of their
money. In fact, it was how she survived. The only
problem was, Six didn't have time for Sparkle to
romance a nigga for a year in order for them to
share their money with her. Free had six months
to come up with a quarter million. Six knew that
they would have to take it by any means necessary. There wouldn't be enough time for the
lovey-dovey approach; Sparkle would have to
lure them into a situation where Free could hit
their pockets for big cash. The money would get
split three equal ways and after a couple licks
they should have enough money to pay Claude
and leave town. She paced the same back-and-
forth pattern for an hour trying to piece together
her plan before Free walked in the door, interrupting her train of thought.

Six could see the tension in Free's face. She
walked over to him and kissed him softly on the
lips. He rested his forehead on hers and wrapped
his arms around her waist, placing his hands
on her round behind. She rubbed the back of

his head and watched as he closed his eyes and sighed heavily. She could tell that the financial burdens that they were in were dampening his spirit. She wanted to tell Free about her plan, but she didn't know what he would think. She was sure that her plan would work. Everybody who frequented the club had major chips to play with. They made it a point to show it off. Why not take advantage of their stupidity and rob them blind? Six didn't want Free to think that she had ever entertained the thought of hustling niggas while he was away so she hesitated in telling him about her idea. He knew the type of stuff that went on inside the Kitty Kat, which is one reason why he hated the fact that she worked there.

"Why are you so quiet?" he asked her as he looked into her eyes. He could read her like a book and could tell that something was on her mind. "What are you thinking about?"

"Everything. I'm thinking about all of this," she began softly. "We are in some serious shit, Free. We need to come up with a quarter mil in six months. What type of hustle you know turning that type of profit?" she asked him.

"Moving weight . . . but I think I'm stuck with that. I'm not trying to go back to prison. They'll put me in a box before they stick me in there again," Free whispered.

"I know," Six said as she grabbed his hands and intertwined her fingers with his.

"I think I know a way for us to get this money," Six announced. Free didn't respond; he just listened and waited for her to continue.

"You know all them niggas be flashing big money down at the club, right? Well, I say we set them up to be robbed. Sparkle always got some chump from the club spending money on her and telling her his business. Why not use her to help us get the dough? She can approach them, spend a couple days with them . . . she knows exactly what to do to find out anything we need to know. She can find out where they stash spots at or when and where the pickup is. Next thing you know, she leads them to a hotel or secluded spot and we take the money. It'll be quick and easy; nobody will get hurt," Six said as her eyes pleaded with Free, hoping he would go along with her plan.

"So you wanna pimp your friend?" Free asked with uncertainty and contempt.

"Free, please don't give me that. You already know how she gets down. Sparkle pimps herself anyway, so it doesn't make a difference. We might as well get paid from it. Besides, we'll split the money up three ways, but me and you are together, so in actuality, we'll be getting the bigger percentage. It'll be a sixty-five—thirty-five split, and she's the one who's doing most of the work. We can't lose, baby. She'll never notice that we are taking home most of the money."

Free's mind was spinning. The plan sounded good in theory, but he wasn't sure if he wanted to get involved in something so risky. He didn't trust Sparkle enough to get in bed with her on a setup. "I don't know, Six." He had seen that shit catch up to a couple dudes in the hood.

"Baby, this is the only way. I went to see my daddy today and he told me that the best way to get to a man is through his woman. We make Sparkle get to them for us. After a couple times we should have the money we need to pay our debt."

Free thought about what Six had just proposed. In a way the plan was brilliant. He couldn't believe that she had come up with the entire plan in a day's time. He knew that what she was saying was true. He had seen Sparkle work her magic on plenty of hustlers, but he also knew that when she was through with them they were almost ready to kill her. He didn't want to pull Six into a game that was so uncertain. Anything could easily go wrong during a stickup and he didn't want her involved in it. She was his life and this was his debt; she had done enough by even coming up with the hustle. He didn't see why she had to be involved in it.

"Six, I don't want you wrapped up in this. Me and Sparkle can handle it."

"What?"

"If anything ever happened to you I would go crazy, Six. I don't need that on my mind if we are going to do this."

"No, Free! You are not cutting me out of this plan. You always think about how you would feel if something happened to me. What about how I'm going to feel if something happens to you? You left me once and that is not going to happen again. Whatever happens it's going to happen to both of us. We are in this together. If you go to jail, I go to jail. If you die, I die."

Free shook his head, but eventually relented because Six was not going to take no for an answer. Once her mind was set there was no changing it. If it was going to be done then it was going to be done together. He couldn't believe what he had gotten her into. Here she was plotting money schemes when all she should have to be worried about was living good and making their lives happy. Guilt filled his heart as he looked at his queen. *When I'm back on top, she will never want for anything. I'm gon' spoil her,* he thought.

He knew that he had a thoroughbred on his team. Six stuck by his side through the worst of times when the average female would have blown in the wind. No matter what he was going through she was always there. When he first started hustling she chose to be with him when other cats were talking about how much they could do for her. When he made it to the top she rightfully took her place as his woman. She was the ghetto princess of the hood and the baddest bitch in Detroit. She knew her role and was the woman behind the man. When he fell off she was there to pick him up. She stuck by him during his three-year stay in prison and would have done the entire fifteen to life if she had to. Now he was out and in a deadly confrontation with his connect and she stood by him still, proving her loyalty beyond a doubt. He was in love with her and at that moment he remembered why.

"So are we in or out?" she asked him with her neatly arched eyebrows raised.

"We're in," he answered. "Have you talked to Sparkle about any of this?" he asked.

"No, not yet."

Free had a look of confusion on his face before he inquired, "Well, how do you know she will be down for it?"

"Oh, you don't know Sparkle. If it's about money, she'll be with it."

Free nodded in agreement. Sparkle was a professional gold digger. She had so many niggas buying her things and paying her bills that they were hard to count. She didn't even really need her job at the strip club. She only kept it so that she could be in tune with who was getting money. She was good at what she did, and if all went as planned, Free knew that they would all be rolling in money very soon.

Sparkle turned around, shook her ass at the crowd, and they went crazy. She was five feet three and had the body of a goddess. Her wide hips and big breasts wore the thong and stilettos well as she gave the performance of her life. She rolled her hips and popped her assets as she watched the dollar bills flood the stage. The patrons of the club loved when Sparkle hit the stage. She was by far the freakiest stripper in the club, and niggas knew that there were no limitations to what she could or would do. As long as the compensation was sufficient, she was down for whatever, and she was known for giving the best head in town. Free watched Sparkle as she seductively trotted around on the stage and noticed that the audience was devouring her every move. All eyes were fixated on Sparkle and the gold pasties that she wore on each nipple. Sparkle was a pro, and she scanned the crowd with efficiency, trying to see what chump she would make their first mark.

Six's stomach felt like it was doing somersaults. She was nervous as hell and didn't know what was going to happen. She hoped that her plan was 100 percent and that she hadn't overlooked something important. She glanced toward the back of the club where Free was sitting. He was so far in the back that he was hidden by the shadows of the abandoned section of the club. All of the other patrons were crowded around the stage but Six knew that Free was watching his surroundings, trying to be as cautious as possible.

Sparkle spotted one of the regulars out of the crowd. Drake came to the club every Saturday night and always had a fat knot in his pocket. He stayed fresh and drove a white Escalade on spinners. When he was in the club he always made it rain and she smiled enticingly at him, knowing that he was the one she was about to get at. He winked at her and when her set was finished he motioned for her to join him at a table in the corner.

"What's good with you li'l bit?" he asked her, calling her by one of her many club names.

"What's good with you?" she replied as she licked her lips and made herself comfortable, straddling his lap. His hands instantly found her backside.

"I'm trying to find out where the party at after this," he told her as he moved her G-string out of the way and slipped one of his fingers into her womanhood. She rotated on it, causing his fingers to become drenched in her wetness. His boys were sitting around the table enjoying the mini freak show that the two were putting on but Sparkle didn't care. Her attention was focused on getting in Drake's pockets. Reaching her hands in the pockets of his Sean John jeans, she felt the thick wad of bills rolled in a rubber band, but bypassed it and began to stroke his hard dick. He thought that she was trying to please him, but what she was really doing was probing his pockets to make sure he had money on him. She felt another wad in his other pocket and dollar signs formed in her eyes. Slyly, she looked over at Free and nodded her head to signal him that she was ready and her eyes followed him as he got up and walked out the club.

"You already found the party, sweetie," she told Drake as she probed in his jeans and felt how hard he really was.

"You gon' let cha boy get in that?" he asked as he continued to finger her as she sat on his lap.

"You can do whatever you want if the money is right. I get off in an hour and I've got a room. *If* your money is proper we can head that way," she told him, emphasizing the *if*, letting him know that if he wasn't paid he wasn't getting laid.

He nodded and called a waitress over to the table. "Bring me a bottle of Cris," he announced as he pulled one of the money wads out of his pocket. He handed the waitress two hundred-dollar bills and as he turned to Sparkle he held the money in her face and said, "The money is always right."


Free sped to the closest motel, which was about ten miles from the club. He pulled into the Holiday Inn and parked his car. He was glad that Six had to work that night because he didn't want her leaving the club trying to come with him their first time. He rushed into the hotel, paid cash for the room, and then got two keys. *I hope this shit goes smooth, I ain't trying to catch a body if some shit pop off,* Free thought as he drove back to the strip club. He went in and headed to the bar where Six was pouring drinks. They made eye contact and Free slipped the other hotel key behind the bar. She nodded and continued what she was doing without even speaking to him. He then left the club to prepare himself for what was about to go down.

Thirty minutes later, Sparkle sashayed out of the dressing room fully clothed with a huge smile plastered on her face. She greeted Drake with a kiss and led him over to the bar.

"One more shot before we hit the road," Sparkle said. Six wiped down the bar as she watched Sparkle whisper into Drake's ear.

"The bar is about to close, so can I get you guys anything?" Six asked, pretending that she didn't know Sparkle.

"Two shots of Patrón," Sparkle responded.

Six prepared the drinks and discreetly slipped a white substance into Drake's before handing it to him. She sighed in relief when she saw him consume the liquor. She knew that the hit would go smoothly because once the date Rohypnol kicked in, Drake would be an easy target.

Sparkle overpaid for the drink, and Six slid the hotel key in with her change, then watched the couple walk out the club. Sparkle got into his truck, and he immediately reached up her skirt. "Where the room at?" he asked. Sparkle smiled at his frankness. He was drunk and horny, exactly how she needed him to be. She unbuckled his belt and unzipped the fly to his jeans. His manhood stood at attention, and she lowered her head to wrap her lips around him. He went crazy as she worked her tongue and when he hit a bump, his dick slid all the way to the back of her throat, making him scream out loud.

"Damn, girl!"

Sparkle gave him head all the way to the hotel, and when he finally parked, he was ready to sex her right there in the car. He pulled his seat back and grabbed her forcefully, pulling her onto his exposed penis. She moaned as he slipped easily into her and she started to grind him hard.

"Wait, let's take this up to the room," she whispered seductively, remembering the real reason why she had come to the motel. She led the way up to room 946 and walked in and turned on the light. Slowly she slipped out of her clothes and revealed a red thong and bra set.

"Hold up, I need to freshen up," she said as she walked into the bathroom and locked the door behind her. She pulled the shower curtain back to find Free standing there with his finger on his lips, signaling for her to be quiet. Her heart was pumping, and she was beginning to get nervous.

"What now?" she asked him in a whisper that was almost inaudible.

"Do what you would do if I wasn't here," he whispered back, "and I'll take care of the rest," and closed the shower curtain. Sparkle flushed the toilet and just as she opened the door to leave, Drake rushed in.

"Move, girl, I got to piss," he said as he brushed past her and closed the door on a fear-filled Sparkle.

Free peeked through the crack of the shower curtain and had his gun aimed and ready just in case Drake had heard him or discovered his hiding spot. He watched as Drake opened up a bottle of Valtrex and turned on the water and swallowed a pill. Free almost burst out laughing as he watched Drake take the pill, then pull out his penis and examine it. *This nasty mu'fucka got herpes,* Free thought as he smirked and shook his head. Drake finished handling his business and walked out of the bathroom.

Sparkle breathed a sigh of relief when she saw Drake return to the room with a smile on his face. She thought that she was caught but he hadn't discovered Free so their plan was still in motion. She took off all his clothes and then went to the bed where she spread her legs wide open, waiting for him to enter her. He entered her slowly and she moaned loudly to let Free know that she was ready. Drake was in mid-hump when Free came out of the bathroom and hit him on the back of his head with the butt of his gun. Drake yelled out in pain as he turned around and was greeted by a masked Free, pointing a .357-caliber pistol at his dome.

"Let's make it simple. You know what I'm here for," Free said calmly.

Sparkle screamed for dramatic effect and Free slapped the shit out of her too. Her eyes bucked wide and she stumbled as she tried to pick her face up off the floor. Free laughed a little bit. *She wasn't expecting that shit,* he thought.

"I don't have no—"

Before Drake could even get the lie out of his mouth Free pistol-whipped him, causing him to black out.

"Drake! Drake!" Sparkle screamed as she moved his shoulder, trying to play her role but really checking to see if he was out cold. "He's out," she announced as she stood up and wiped the spot of blood that trailed from her lip.

Free reached down and pulled the three large wads of money out of his pockets. Free was good with the cash flow and from the looks of the sizes of the rolls he estimated it to be about fifteen thousand dollars. *Hell, yeah! Six was right.* They both left the hotel and drove toward Free's house.

When they arrived Six was sitting on the couch with her knees tucked into her chest, looking worried. When she saw Free walk in she practically jumped in his arms.

"Are you okay? Did everything go as planned?" she asked as she hugged him and looked back and forth between her man and her best friend. "What happened to your lip?" she asked Sparkle with a frown.

"Ask your boy!" she blurted out as she rolled her eyes at Free and felt the swell of her lip.

Free shrugged and said, "I had to make it look realistic." Six punched Free softly in the chest and laughed a little bit under her breath. "How much did we get?" was her next question.

Free sat down and pulled the first rubber band off the money. He anxiously flipped through the bills. He peeled off the first bill and began counting, "fifty . . . fifty-one, fifty-two, fifty-three . . ." Free frowned up and stared up at Six. He kept flipping through the money to find that there were only one-dollar bills. He quickly unraveled the two other wads and found the same thing.

"This frontin'-ass nigga had dollar bills wrapped up with a fifty on top. Fuck! We just robbed this mu'fucka for three hundred dollars!" He threw the bills toward the wall, and they floated in the air until they met their resting place on the living room floor. Free was pissed; he had just gotten involved in an armed robbery for some petty cash. "I thought you said he was paid!" he yelled loudly as he pointed in Sparkle's face.

"I thought he was! He always at the club throwing money around and talking about what he got and how much he's moving weight. How was I supposed to know the nigga was fugazzi?" she said as she yelled back at Free and looked at Six to back her up.

"She's right, Free, there's no way we could have known," Six said.

"Fuck this shit . . . I'm out! Y'all can keep that three hundred dollars. Call me when y'all ready to hit a nigga with big pockets," Sparkle said as she walked out of the apartment, still nursing her busted lip. Free rubbed his hands over his low-cut caesar and hit the wall with his fist out of frustration. Six looked at the dollar bills that were scattered on the floor.

Free was upset right now, but she knew that they needed every dollar they could get, no matter how small the amount. She put her pride aside as tears built up in her eyes, then he bent down and began to pick up the money from the floor.

# Chapter Four

Britain "Brick" Adams slowly pulled onto the avenue in a tinted Lexus Coupe. His deep chocolate skin tone blended in perfectly with his chocolate Sean John suit, which was accented by a mocha-colored shirt and tie. His neat caesar haircut and stubble facial hair gave him the best of both worlds, making him look neat but still rugged at the same time. Britain squinted his eyes, trying to remember what the house he was searching for looked like. He spotted Jones's house and unloosened his tie.

"I hate these damn ties," he said to himself as he thought about how he had to dress accordingly for his court hearing. He had just left the court concerning his illegal affairs and the prosecuting DA was painting him to be worse than Nino Brown.

As he turned into Jones's driveway, he saw a young woman leaving Jones's house, and he couldn't help but to admire her beauty. As he looked closer, he couldn't believe his eyes. She looked very familiar to him. When he looked deeper into her facial features, he knew exactly who she was.

"Is that Six?" he asked, remembering her from childhood. "I thought she lived in New York." Britain noticed that she had filled out nicely since he had last seen her. He hadn't seen her in roughly fifteen years, when she used to come down and visit her father for the summer. Britain's father and Jones used to be crime partners back in the day. That was before Britain's father, also nicknamed Brick, was murdered during a botched robbery. Jones was present and held Britain's father in his arms as he left this earth.

Britain quickly snapped out of his daydream and watched as Six pulled off. He was there to see Jones, who he hadn't talked to in over five years. Ever since Britain's heroin business had expanded, he strayed away from Jones, who was his mentor and godfather. Britain stepped out of his car and introduced his expensive Mauri gators to the pavement. He walked up to the door and knocked on it at the same rhythm he always did.

Moments later, Jones came to the door with a big smile on his face and a tightly rolled joint hanging from the right side of his mouth.

"Li'l Brick! Come here, boy," Jones said as he pulled the grown man close to him as if he was a little boy.

"Jones! What's up, old man? Long time no see," Britain said as they unlocked their strong embrace and he stepped into the house.

"Old man? It ain't nothing about me old, youngblood. Better ask that twenty-one-year-old I had over here last night," Jones said playfully as he smoothly strolled over to his couch and sat down. "Have a seat," he demanded.

"Thanks," Britain said humbly as he took a seat directly in front of him.

"To what did I owe this visit?" Jones asked as one of his eyes closed while lighting up the Mary Jane.

"OG, I been going through some shit lately," Britain said as he sat back and rested his hands on his lap.

"I know, I know. I've been seeing that shit on CNN for the past month now. They are making you out to be a damn monster. Drug kingpin! Killer! Every other word that bitch Nancy Grace is calling you is something negative," Jones said just before he took a deep, slow pull of his joint.

"Tell me about it," Britain said as he shook his head in disgust at the way the media was portraying him. Although he was a heroin kingpin, he wasn't a monster. He never killed anyone who didn't have it coming, and he was a very loyal person. He was from the ghetto of Detroit, where the success rate was very low for a black male, and he did what he had to do to come up. "They don't have a strong case against me. It's only one thing that has me worried," Britain confessed to Jones.

"What's that?" Jones asked, trying to get a better understanding of what Britain was getting at.

Britain leaned in close to Jones, as if he was sharing a secret or someone was listening in on them. "They got a witness that supposed to testify against me," he said.

"Damn," Jones huffed as he thought about snitch niggas. "What does he know?" Jones said in a lowered tone, matching Britain's.

"Everything," Britain said in a frustrated whisper. "He used to run packs for me. I took the nigga under my wing, showed him how to get money, and he turned on me."

"I hate snitches!" Jones said as he shook his head from side to side.

"He's singing like a bird, Jones."

"When is he supposed to testify?" Jones asked, trying to help Britain sort out his little problem.

"In one month exactly," Britain responded.

"Well, you know what you got to do. It's just that simple," Jones said as he flicked the ashes into his ashtray.

"It's not that easy. The feds got him in custody. That's why I came to you," Britain said as he looked Jones dead in the eyes.

"Oh, no, youngblood. I retired years ago. I can't move around like I used to. That's a young man's job, ya dig?" Jones stated.

"I know, I know. But I have to have this done right. By one of the best," Britain said, trying to urge Jones to come out of retirement.

"I know where you getting at, but I stepped out of the murder game ten years ago," Jones said.

"You know I wouldn't have come to you unless I really needed you. The feds got all of my associates under a microscope, and I can't make a move. I need an outside source to take care of this one for me. I need that end clipped, nah mean?" Britain said as he reached into his pocket and pulled out an envelope. "This is just in case you have a change of heart. It's the picture, location, and rundown of the snitch. He is being held just outside the city under the FBI's watch. Just to throw it out there . . . I'm paying a quarter mil for his head. His name is Jermaine Harris. I only need the snitch hit, nothing more, nothing less."

"Damn—a quarter million?" Jones stated in surprise.

"My freedom is worth that," Britain replied seriously.

Jones picked up the envelope and thought hard before he gave Britain a final no. Immediately, a lightbulb popped in Jones's head, and he began to think about Free. He knew that Free used to put his murder game down before he went to prison and was more than qualified for the job. "I'm not fucking with it. But I think I know someone who is perfect for the contract. I'm pretty sure he can handle it, and he needs the money. I vouch for him," Jones said, thinking about Free's potential comeup.

"Okay. Just please get it done for me," Britain said as he stood up and held out his hand. Jones also stood up and then shook Britain's hand. Britain headed toward the door, but stopped just before he opened it and stepped out. "Was that Six that was leaving when I pulled up?" he asked.

"Yeah, that was her. Y'all used to fight like cats and dogs growing up. I'm surprised you still remember her," Jones stated.

*I remember her, all right,* Britain thought, remembering what he had seen earlier. She had a beautiful shape, and he told himself that if he saw her again, he would make sure to reintroduce himself.

"Later, Jones," Britain said before he exited.

Jones picked up the phone, and made a call to Free. He had a great opportunity for him.

Free sat in front of Jones, looking at the surveillance pictures of the snitch being escorted into a small safe house. Free was thrilled, knowing that he was about to come into some major money.

"The only problem is that he is guarded by the feds," Jones added as he licked the rolling paper after he completed rolling up a doobie.

"The feds?" Free asked as he sat back and looked at Jones as if he was crazy.

"Yeah. I'm not saying you should take it, but it sure is good money."

Free thought long and hard about his situation and figured he had nothing to lose. If he didn't pay back the Russians, he was as good as dead and he had to go all in. Desperate times called for desperate measures and that statement couldn't have been truer in this situation.

"Fuck it! I'ma hit 'em. How much he paying again?" Free double-checked.

"A quarter mil. However, I'm taking twenty-five percent. Ya know, in commission fees."

"Twenty-five percent? Damn, Jones! What happen to ten to fifteen percent for commissions?" Free asked, giving Jones a slight grin.

"Baby, this is the streets. This ain't no real estate deal. Jones got to eat, baby!" he said charmingly as he smiled back and took a pull of the joint.

"I feel you. I feel you. You are a stone-cold hustler, you know that?" Free said as he admired the bluntness and savvy of the man sitting in front of him who was thirty years his senior. They both shook hands, and Free gathered all the information back into the envelope before slipping it into his inside coat pocket. He was about to get on his hustle; murder for hire was the name of the game.

# Chapter Five

Free and Big Lou sat in the tinted Dodge Charger and watched the silhouettes of the men that moved around within the house. They were deep in the suburbs in the city of Oak Park, just outside Detroit's city limits. They were staked out discreetly a couple of houses down from the safe house where the agents were guarding Jermaine. The curtains were closed so they couldn't see exactly how many people were in the house, but they knew that Jermaine was inside because of the information that Britain had supplied Jones with. They had been watching the house nonstop for the past four days and were waiting for a small slip so that they could hit Britain's snitch.

"This shit is useless. We're just wasting our damn time," Lou complained as he eyed the door in frustration. Free slowly put his hand up, almost as if he was gesturing Lou to calm down.

"Trust me, Lou. We just have to be patient, feel me?" Free asked with confidence. Just as

Lou opened his mouth to respond, a car pulled up to the house. Free instantly sat up and looked closer at the vehicle that pulled into the driveway of the spot. After a couple of seconds, a skinny teen jumped out of the car with three boxes of pizza while his car was left running.

"Them mu'fuckas forever ordering pizzas," Lou said as he leaned his head back in the headrest. Free watched as the kid went to the door and knocked. The same man opened the door and took the pizza, just as he did the past couple of nights. Free noticed that the well-built white man had a gun on his waist and his shiny badge was noticeable from a mile away.

"I wonder how many agents are in there?" Free asked as he rubbed his chin, trying to sort things out in his head.

"Don't know. But how we going to get to this nigga when he guarded by the feds? We can't just go in blasting. That would be suicide," Lou exclaimed. Free slowly grew a smile on his face as he got an idea on how they could get in to the snitch.

"What the fuck you got up your sleeve?" Lou asked as he noticed the sudden change in Free's facial expression.

"I got a plan," Free said as he watched the pizza man take money from the agent and head back to his car.

***

Two days later, once again, Free and Big Lou were waiting patiently a couple of houses down from the safe house.

"Bingo," Lou whispered as he saw the same car pull up that had come two days earlier. Lou and Free cocked their guns back at the same time and then pulled the ski masks over their face, only exposing their eyes and lips. They both jumped out of the car and crept up on the pizza delivery guy as he approached the porch. Free snatched him back just before he put one foot on the steps that led to the safe house.

"Aghhh," the unsuspecting teen yelled as he didn't know what hit him.

Free quickly put his hand over the teen's mouth and pulled him to the side of the house where Lou's big ass was crouched down.

"Listen, little nigga," Free whispered harshly as he placed the cold steel on the teen's neck. "If you do what I say, everything is going to be okay." Free pulled his hand from over the boy's mouth and waited for a response. The boy still had the pizza boxes in his hands and was sweating like a hooker in church. He was nervous as hell and didn't know what was going on. He nodded in agreement, and Free and Lou smiled, knowing that they were about to make the contract money.

*Knock, knock, knock.*

Free's back was against the wall next to the front door, and he had the loaded black .45 pointed directly at the pizza boy's head. "Stay calm," Free whispered to the boy, coaching him through the process. The boy tried to swallow, but it seemed like he had an apple in his throat and sweat began to drip down his face as he didn't know what to expect.

Seconds later, an agent came to the door with a gun in hand, but when he saw the pizza boy, he put his gun in his waist and asked, "How much I owe you?"

Before the pizza boy could answer, Free emerged and placed his gun on the temple of the agent.

"Get out of here, li'l man," Free whispered as he turned his head in the direction of the car. Without hesitation, the boy dropped the pizza boxes and took off, scared shitless. Free then pulled the agent out of the house and put his lips on the agent's ear, so that he could hear him clearly.

"I'ma ask you this one time and one time only. If you lie, I'ma blow yo' top off. How many people are in there?"

"Look, you don't know what you're getting yourself into, son," the agent suggested as he had both of his hands up in the air. Free didn't have time to play with the agent, so he struck him in the head with the butt of the gun, causing him to fall to the ground. Then he reached in to the agent's holster and grabbed his gun. Free tossed his gun to Lou and once again put his gun to the agent's head.

"You got one more time, homeboy," Free said as he clenched his jaws and pressed the barrel to the man's head.

As blood leaked from the agent's mouth, he mumbled, "Four of us are in there. Plus the witness is in the back," he admitted as he realized that Britain had sent someone for Jermaine.

Free grabbed him by the collar and picked him up. Then he stood behind him and placed the gun to the back of his head as he directed him into the house. When Free entered the house, the smell of cigar smoke invaded his nostrils and he noticed that the agents were sitting at a poker table with cards in their hands. They didn't even notice Free approaching with their buddy in his grasp.

Without even looking, one of the agents said jokingly, "Johnson, what took you so long? You give the pizza man a blow job," he asked, and everyone burst into laughter. But all the laughing stopped when they looked at Johnson and noticed that he had his hands up with an armed masked man behind him.

One of the agents tried to reach for his gun that was on the table, but Free quickly pointed his gun at him and said, "Slow ya row," causing him to put both of his hands up. Free quickly grabbed the gun off the table and placed it in his waist, just before putting the gun back on the man.

"Fuck!" one of the agents yelled as he threw his cards down. He knew that they had just been caught slipping. Their holsters and guns were on the other side of the room, and he knew that they were screwed.

"Everybody, hands up," Free directed as he saw someone dart through the hallway and out the back door. Free smiled, knowing that it was Jermaine. Only seconds later, Lou was bringing Jermaine back in the house from the rear. Free had already anticipated that he would do that, so he had Lou waiting at the back door for him.

"Nice of you to join us," Free said as he smiled inside his mask. He kicked the agent down to his knees and went into his hoodie and pulled out zip-ties and tied his hands behind his back. He grabbed each agent and made them follow suit. Then he put duct tape around their mouths. He lined all of them up on their knees and tied all of them securely. That's when he focused his attention on Jermaine while Lou had him at gunpoint.

Jermaine was shaking nervously, knowing that his life was about to end. He figured he had nothing to lose so he swung around and knocked Lou's gun on the ground. They began to tussle and Free couldn't get a good aim on Jermaine to shoot him as they wrestled each other.

In the midst of all the commotion, Jermaine ripped Lou's ski mask off and exposed his face. Free ran over to them as they fell onto the ground and then Free struck Jermaine in the back of his head, causing him to become temporarily dizzy. This gave Lou enough time to regain his composure.

"You can't handle this li'l nigga?" Free yelled as he watched Jermaine on the floor holding the back of his bleeding head. Free couldn't believe how Lou let Jermaine get the best of him, especially knowing that Lou had him beat by at least 100 pounds plus.

"Fuck!' Lou yelled as he searched for his ski mask on the ground. Once he found it, he put it back on his head, but at that point, it was too late because the agents had seen his face.

Lou gave Jermaine a hard kick to the face, landing him flat on his back. Free was tired of playing and without hesitation gave Jermaine two slugs to the chest. He stared down at Jermaine and watched as blood leaked from his mouth and his body began to shake. Jermaine was fighting for his life as his body twitched, and he began to choke on his own blood. Free, wanting to put Jermaine out of his misery, gave him another bullet. Only that time, Jermaine stopped moving altogether. The bullet to the head rocked him to sleep forever.

Free looked at Big Lou and shook his head in disappointment. Lou dropped his head, knowing that he was slipping and not on his A-game that night. Free could hear the whimpering of one agent as tears formed in his eyes. It always amazed Free how a man who seemed so tough could bitch up in the face of death.

Free walked behind the agents and without hesitation shot each of them with a slug to the back of their domes. He had no choice; he had to turn what was supposed to be a homicide into a ruthless massacre. Lou had exposed his face, and he had to do what he had to do. The bodies dropped like dominoes as Free went down the line hitting each one of them with a bullet that wasn't meant for them.

"Let's roll," Free instructed as he stepped over the corpses and headed for the door. He had just fulfilled the contract on the snitch's head, and he could already feel the money in his palms.

\*\*\*

"I can't believe this shit," Britain whispered under his breath as he and one of his goons watched CNN while sitting on his sectional.

"Four federal agents and the star witness in the Britain 'Brick' Adams case were found murdered execution-style in a home in Oak Park. Authorities are saying that this was a contract kill and Adams is suspected to be behind this heinous act. More details are soon to come as we cover this story that is turning out to be just like a scene out of *The Sopranos*."

Britain turned off the television, not wanting to hear any more of the fiasco that was unraveling.

Veins poked from his neck as he clenched his jaws, displaying his rage. His BlackBerry had been ringing off the hook because of the recent events. He knew that nine times out of ten his phone was being tapped, so he never picked up. His teams of lawyers were working overtime trying to figure out the next step. However, the district attorney was irate now that his star witness was dead. Jermaine was the only thing that tied Britain to the drug-trafficking charges. Things were looking very bad for Britain, and he knew that he had to go and see Jones to find out what went wrong.

"Damn!" he yelled as he threw his remote at the TV, cracking the screen of his five-thousand-dollar plasma TV. Britain got up and grabbed his coat. He was going straight to Jones and see what was going on.

"Yo, meet me in the garage," Britain said as he instructed his goon to go to the garage through the house. He was going to go in the car garage from the outside, so that he could do a magic trick for the feds who were watching him. Just as he was stepping out, he saw two men in trench coats and suits approaching his door. By the way they looked, Britain knew they were cops. There was something about being a cop that was evident, and Britain knew all the signs.

"I was just on my way out, fellas," Britain said calmly as he stopped in his tracks and slid his hands in his pockets.

"Fuck you, you son of a bitch," one of the agents said as his face became as red as a fresh apple. "Johnson was a father and a good guy. I'm going to put you in a cage for the rest of your life," the agent promised as he lunged at Britain while his partner held him back. Britain didn't even budge. He just looked at the man like it was a joke. However, inside, Britain was steaming mad. He never knew Jones to be so sloppy, and he regretted even giving him the contract.

"Well, if this li'l charade is over . . . I have somewhere to be," Britain said as he walked past the men.

"Hey, we need to talk to you," the cop said as he pointed his finger at Britain.

"You can talk to my lawyer. Now, if you don't have a warrant, you might want to get off my mu'fuckin' property before I get upset," Britain said as he displayed a small smile, but it quickly turned into a scowl to let them know he was dead serious.

The agents brushed past Britain and got into their car. Britain watched as they pulled off. He waited until they were out of sight and then headed over to Jones's house to talk to the man who just threw salt in the game. Once the cops were out of eyesight, Britain went to his garage that was attached to his house. He stepped in and pressed the button so he could let the door down. He had six cars in the spacious garage and decided to get into his Cadillac truck. He then watched as his goon got into the tinted Benz.

"Just circle around the block for a minute. Keep 'em busy," Britain instructed as he started up his truck and rolled up the windows, which were also tinted. He pushed the garage-door opener to let the door up.

His goon pulled out and just as Britain suspected, a black unmarked police car was camped out a couple of houses down.

Britain sat across from Jones shaking his head in disbelief. Jones was just as shocked as Britain when he saw the news on CNN.

"How dumb can a nigga be?" Jones asked as an unlit joint hung from the right side of his mouth.

Britain got up and began to pace the room while in deep contemplation.

"Well, at least they did hit the snitch," Jones said as he lit the joint, trying to make light of the situation. He sat back in his La-Z-Boy and began to think about the commission that Free had just blown for him. He knew Britain was not going to pay for a botched hit. Jones fully understood. However, Free might not take the news so easily.

"Yeah, but what good does that do? I'm going to have the feds gunning for me. Four of their own were murdered execution-style with a witness that was set to take the stand against *me*!"

"Listen, youngblood. I take full responsibility for this mishap. My man fucked up the job," Jones stated.

"It's cool. This just fucks everything up though," Britain said as he calmed down. Jones was a man who he always looked up to, and he had to remember that he was talking to an OG.

A knock on the door interrupted their conversation. Jones put out his joint and went to answer the door. It was Free. Jones stepped to the side to let him in, and Free had a smile on his face, thinking he was coming to collect.

"What's going on, Jones?" Free asked as he stepped in. He looked at Britain and nodded, but Britain didn't acknowledge him back. Free smirked and shook his head as he walked past Britain.

"So what's up?" Free asked as he sat down. He was ready to collect and go to see Claude to pay some of his debt off. Free watched as Britain began to slowly pace the room with his hands in his pocket, noticeably angry.

"We got a problem, Free. Why did you take out the agents? That fucked it up for everybody," Jones said as he sat back down in his chair and looked across at Free.

"I had to. They saw my man's face," Free said as he put his hands out.

"Damn. You didn't have to kill them, though," Jones responded.

"Of course, I did. Think about it," Free said, trying to get Jones to see things his way. Jones was a hit man and knew the rules of the game, which was "no witness, no murder."

"Jones, the contract is all fucked up. I'm not paying," Britain said as he looked at Jones. Jones nodded in agreement, knowing that his reasoning was fair.

"What? You ain't paying? You got me fucked up," Free said as he sat up and looked at Britain like he was crazy. "Yo', man tripping," he said as he looked at Jones.

"You better calm down, li'l nigga," Britain said as he raised his shirt, exposing his nickel-plated .45-caliber pistol.

"Look, everybody, relax," Jones said as he stood up, trying to keep the peace. Free had heard enough. He was furious. He couldn't believe that he wasn't getting paid for his services, but he had another plan in mind. He was going to make Britain pay one way or another.

"It's cool. Later, Jones," Free said as he stormed out, putting a plot together in his head. He was back at square one.

# Chapter Six

Six heard the front door slam, so she walked into the living room where she found Free and Big Lou. She could immediately sense that something was wrong. The thick tension that filled the air could be cut with a knife, and Free's agitation was written all over his face. His temple throbbed from emotion as he grit his teeth in anger.

"What's wrong?" She asked as she approached Free with open arms. He kissed her cheek as she stroked his face. Stress lines creased his forehead, but he didn't respond . . . choosing to ignore her question. She looked from Free to Big Lou in search of answers. "Free? What's up? Where's the money?"

Six was sure that Free would come back with a duffel bag full of big faces, but as she looked at his empty hands, she was confused.

"There is no money," Free stated as he sat down on the couch. "That bitch-ass nigga Britain pulled grimy."

"Why would he do that? That nigga is sitting on money. . . . Why would he not pay you after you put in work for him?" Six asked.

"Things didn't go as planned, but the nigga got me fucked up if he think he gon' chump me out of that paper. The mu'fucka wasn't even on my radar before this, but he's going to pay me what he owes me . . . one way or another."

"What you got in mind?" Big Lou asked.

"I'ma take it out his ass," Free stated harshly . . . irrationally, letting his anger hype him up.

"I'm with it, but the nigga ain't easy to touch. If we gone come at him, we need to come correct, because he stay strapped, and he got eyes on him at all times," Big Lou said.

"So you're saying the nigga untouchable?" Free asked.

"No, I'm saying the nigga ain't your average mark. If we rob him, we better be ready to kill him, because he's not taking L's in stride. Don't let that suit-wearing shit fool you. The nigga is ruthless and got an army of goons standing behind him," Big Lou said.

"So we kidnap his bitch and tie up his kid until the nigga cough up that cake," Free stated mercilessly. He didn't care how he got paid as long as he did. Free was a stand-up man with those who were loyal and played fairly with him, but Britain had disrespected him so he fully intended on settling the score.

"Nah, it's not that easy, fam. The nigga don't keep no steady bitches around. I'm all for getting at the nigga, but we got to approach this situation carefully. I don't know about you, but a nigga value the air in his lungs, nah mean?" Big Lou asked. He wanted to make sure Free fully understood the risk that they were about to take by targeting a man of Britain's stature.

Six sat on the couch with her knees pulled into her chest as she watched the exchange between Free and Big Lou. Free had been locked up for a long time, and he didn't know the magnitude of Britain's reign over the streets. He was larger than life, and Six silently feared for Free's wellbeing. Robbing Britain was dangerous, but Six knew that Free's pride would never allow him to back down.

"You're fam, Lou, and I would never drag you into something that I felt like I couldn't handle, so I'm going to be straight up with you. Right now, I don't have anything to lose. I either come at Britain to get this money, or the Russians coming at me. I'm in a lose-lose, my nigga. I don't have a choice, but I understand if you don't want to be involved," Free stated.

"I'm not feeding you to the sharks, fam. I'm in it with you until the caskets drop in the dirt, but if we can avoid that route, let's be smart. Let's come up with a plan to get at this nigga so that he won't see it coming. Let's not give him time to react," Big Lou replied.

"Put Sparkle on him," Six spoke up.

Free looked at her skeptically and shook his head, but Six was persistent. "I've seen her work a nigga until his pockets were on E. Free, she can do this, and it's the safest way for everyone involved. Nobody has to get hurt. Let it be about the money. We take the cash, pay the Russians, and leave the city."

"A'ight, fuck it. . . . We'll put your girl on him," Free stated.

"He owns a restaurant in Southfield. He has breakfast there every Sunday with his people," Big Lou said.

"You and Sparkle will be there too then," Free said to Six. "Call her and put her up on game. We don't have time to waste."

Six and Sparkle walked into the restaurant looking as if they had stepped right off the pages of a magazine. They were both dressed to impress, and as they waited to be seated, they grabbed the attention of many of the patrons. Free had gone to the restaurant a half hour earlier. He was sipping coffee in a discreet corner of the room. He wanted to see how everything played out, and he grinned as he watched Six and Sparkle captivate the room.

Sparkle smiled, and as they were escorted to their table, they walked past Britain and his entourage. Both of the ladies put on a show, allowing the natural sway of their hips to hypnotize anyone who might be looking. Smiling, they took a seat and opened their menus. Sparkle kicked Six underneath the table and leaned in to whisper, "I'ma hook this nigga so quick he won't know what hit him," she bragged.

Six shook her head and rolled her eyes playfully. "I heard that, bitch. . . . Well, get to work," she said with laughter in her voice. The ladies ordered their food and not even five minutes into their meal the waiter came over.

"Excuse me, ladies. The owner told me to tell you that your meal is on the house, and he asked me to give you this note." The waiter placed a napkin on the table, and Sparkle reached for it.

"Oh, I'm sorry, miss, but the note is for your friend," he said. He handed it directly to Six, who frowned in confusion.

"For me?" she asked.

"Yes, miss, he told me to hand it to you," the waiter replied. "Can I get you anything else?"

Six shook her head, and Sparkle rudely flicked her hand to shoo him away.

"What does the note say?" Sparkle asked nosily.

Six opened the napkin and read:

> *I thought I had everything a man could want, until I saw you.*
> *If you can spare a moment of your time, I'd like to get to know you.*
> *Britain*

Six's cheeks flushed, and her caramel skin looked as if it had been kissed by roses as she balled the note up in her hand.

"What do I do?" Six asked.

"I don't know, but you better figure it out fast because he's walking over here," Sparkle said.

Six looked up just as Britain approached their table. He pulled a chair up and took a seat at the edge, seating himself between the two women.

"This is the second time I've seen you in the past week," Britain stated as he stared her in the eyes. His prestige usually intimidated people, but Six's demeanor was sophisticated, almost arrogant as if she was too good to respond.

"I can't say I recall seeing you the first time," she stated as she continued to eat her food. "What brought you all the way across the restaurant to our table?" she asked.

"A familiar face," he stated. "You don't remember me, but I know you."

Six shook her head and replied, "Nah. You don't know me, but since you're here and you're paying for breakfast, you may as well join us. This is my friend Sparkle, and I'm Six."

Six raised her eyebrows to Sparkle, signaling for her to cut in anytime. Then she stood from the table and dismissed herself. "I'll be right back. I'm going to the ladies' room," she said. Six walked away from the table. She had tried to be as rude as possible to Britain so that it would be easier for Sparkle to charm him. She would give them a minute to converse before rejoining them.

As she walked down the stairs to the bottom level where the restrooms were located, she heard footsteps approach her from behind. She turned around to see Free. He put his hand to his lips and led her to the bathroom where he locked them inside.

"What did he say to you?" Free asked.

"Nothing much . . . just kicking game to me, but that's why I introduced him to Sparkle and left the table. By the time I get back, she should have his full attention," Six explained.

Free shook his head and caressed her face with one hand. "I hope you right, ma, 'cuz from what it looks like, he has his eyes on you."

"She'll get it done. . . . Don't worry. Sparkle knows what she is doing," Six assured. She kissed Free on the lips softly, slowly. "I'm all yours, Free. You'll never have to share," she whispered as he moved from her lips to her neck, his hands roaming all over her body. Her nipples hardened as he continued to kiss her, moving to her shoulders and then her arms. He slipped his hands underneath her dress and found the moisture that was building in between her legs.

"Boy, stop," Six whispered as she squirmed from his touch, a naughty smile spreading across her gorgeous face.

Free got on his knees and lifted her dress, pulling her thong to the side to reveal her juicy pearl. He sucked it into his mouth as if he were sucking on a nipple and molested her jewel with his tongue. Her head fell back, and she closed her eyes. Right there in the bathroom of a crowded restaurant he introduced his woman to ecstasy, bringing her to a quick orgasm.

Afterward, he took a paper towel and cleaned her up. He kissed her cat one last time before pulling down her dress. Then he patted her on the behind and gave her a smile as he waltzed out of the bathroom.

Six took a minute to catch her breath before returning to her table.

"I thought you got lost," Britain said with a smile as he stood up and pulled out her chair.

"Actually, we've got to get going," Six said.

"Is there a way that I can reach you?" Britain asked.

"You don't need to reach me," Six replied with a wink. "Thanks for breakfast, Britain."

She and Sparkle walked out, leaving Britain intrigued. Their plan had backfired. Britain had no interest in Sparkle. He could smell a gold digger from a mile away, but Six he found fascinating. Her entire attitude appealed to him and it was evident to everyone in the room, including Free, that he was checking for her.


"Look, I pulled out all the stops on this one. . . . The nigga must be gay because he wasn't feeling me," Sparkle stated as she paced back and forth in the small living room in Six's apartment. Her ego was crushed, and a twinge of jealousy filled her because she knew that Britain was more attracted to Six.

Free, Big Lou, Six, and Sparkle sat in the living room trying to come up with a way to infiltrate Britain's circle. He had showed absolutely no love for Sparkle, so they knew it would be pointless to try that approach again.

Free looked at Six, who sat in deep thought across from him. He was well aware that she had snagged Britain's attention, and he knew that he could use that to his advantage. His mental wheels began turning as he formulated a plan.

"The nigga feeling you, Six. You're our way in," Free said in a matter-of-fact tone as he stared intensely at her.

"What?" she asked, surprised. She shook her head in defense. "I wouldn't say all that, Free. He can have any girl in this city. He's not worried about me, and I for damn sure ain't thinking about him. Sparkle is our way in," Six stated firmly.

"Come on, Six. I saw the way that he was looking at you. I need you to come off the bench on this one, ma. Get close to the nigga. Make him trust you. Any nigga would be crazy not to want to wife you," Free said.

"Wife me?" Six exclaimed as she looked at Free like he was insane. "Free, I'm not about to share a bed with a nigga like I'm a cheap bitch! Are you crazy?"

"I'm desperate, ma. You know what's going to happen if I don't come up with this loot. It's all or nothing."

"Why me?" Six asked. "Why do I have to be the one to do it? Why can't we just stick to the plan? I'm sure he will warm up to Sparkle eventually."

Big Lou spoke up. "Because the nigga see something in you that he want. You're wifey material. Wifey always has access to the money. . . . If you become that then we're in. All you have to do is play the role."

Tears formed in Six's eyes. She wasn't beyond putting in work, but to rent herself out to another man felt wrong, but then she remembered the Russian men who had invaded her home. She shivered as she remembered the gun that had been placed to her head. She closed her eyes, blinked away the tears, and sighed heavily.

"Please, ma. I need you on this one," Free whispered as he pulled her off the couch, forcing her to sit on his lap. Placing his hand behind her neck, he drew her near for a soft kiss. "I love you, ma. I know you can do this. Do this for me."

"Fine . . . I'll do it," she agreed reluctantly. "What do I have to do?"

"Do the exact same thing that you did to make me love you. You do all that you can to make this nigga trust you, but don't give away what's mine.

Don't fuck the nigga, Six. If it takes all that, it's not worth it," Free instructed.

"Do you really think you have to tell me that?" Six asked. She couldn't believe that she was agreeing to this. It seemed like she was the one who was sacrificing in order to make the money. There was no doubt in her mind that she could get it done, but the fact that Free was asking her to go to such extreme measures bothered her. *Just do it,* she told herself. *After all of this is over with, we can move on with our lives together.*

"How am I supposed to even get at him? I wouldn't even know how to find him again," Six stated.

"The nigga ain't hard to find. He owns a club downtown too," Big Lou revealed.

Six smacked her lips and shook her head in protest. "A nigga like Britain don't want no club-hopping chicken in his face. Y'all said you wanted me to become wifey . . . well, niggas don't meet wifey in the club," she stated.

"I met you in the club," Free countered in irritation. He was frustrated because Six was being too critical of their plan.

"Ha-ha, Free . . . you know what I'm talking about. I didn't come at you on no lovey-dovey–type shit in a club. We met by chance. Y'all niggas know that if a bitch come at you in a club, you probably gon' fuck her that night and never call her again. I can't approach him like that. It'll make me look like a ho, and he'll handle me like one. That's not the way to get to his safe."

Big Lou smirked because he knew Six was right. Most chicks didn't understand the game like she did. She had just laid out the average dude's mental, which is why she would be perfect for the task at hand. She understood how men thought and could use it to her advantage to get Britain to trust her.

Sparkle stood to leave. "Why don't you just go back to the restaurant tomorrow? I'm sure you'll be able to find him there."

Free nodded and looked at Six. "What do you think?" he asked.

She stood to her feet. "Does it really matter what I think?" she asked and began to walk out of the room.

"Where you going, ma? We've still got a lot to talk about," Free said.

"I'm going to lie down. I'm tired . . . we can discuss the details later. I'm in . . . I'll do it . . . for you," Six conceded. Free heard the disheartened tone of her voice and could see the worry in her eyes, but he forced himself to ignore it.

*This is the only way,* he thought as he watched her disappear into the bedroom.

When Six was out of sight, Big Lou leaned forward on the couch, resting his elbows on his knees. He lowered his voice and looked behind him before saying, "You sure you want to do this? This whole thing could blow up in your face . . . you're feeding your main chick to the wolves."

"Think about it, fam . . . do I really have a choice?" Free responded.

"I guess not," Big Lou stated. He slapped hands with Free and then departed with Sparkle, leaving his man to think about what he had just committed his woman to do.

Free knew the risks that were associated with the type of lick he was attempting to pull off. If Britain found out, there was no telling what he would do to Six, but that was the least of Free's worries. When Britain took Six's bait, he would undoubtedly fall for her charm. Free only hoped that Six would hold him down and remain loyal while she was behind enemy lines.

Free joined Six in the bedroom to find that she had already fallen asleep. He sat down beside her and stroked her hair as he watched her chest rise and fall. She was everything to him, and the fact that he was getting ready to loan her to another man made his gut hollow. Just the fact that she had agreed to do it proved her loyalty to him. He kneeled on the floor beside her bed and grabbed her hand in his, planting it with soft kisses. "I love you, ma," he whispered. After everything that they had been through together, he was sure that they could withstand this one last test.

As soon as Six stepped inside the restaurant the next day butterflies began to flutter in her stomach. The stakes were raised for her. Her entire life rested on her own shoulders. If she didn't pull this off, then she could kiss Free good-bye. Her skintight True Religion jeans and red-and-black plaid shirt were meant to be casual, but on a frame like Six's everything seemed provocative. As she waited to be greeted by the host, she shifted her weight from foot to foot, making her behind sway from side to side.

"Table for one, miss?" the host greeted.

She nodded and was led to a table in the rear of the restaurant. Her stilettos made music on the hardwood floor as she walked with the stride of a seasoned model. She sat down, facing the door so that she could see who was coming in and out.

"Is the owner here?" she asked the host before he walked away.

"Yes, he is—is there a problem?" the host asked.

"No, not at all. . . . Could you tell him I would like to speak with him?" Six asked sweetly.

Within minutes, Britain was coming down the wraparound stairs that led to the second level of the establishment. His Usher cologne introduced him before she even saw his face.

She fidgeted with her clothes and took a deep breath as he approached her. He was clad in gray slacks and a Polo sweater with a gray shirt and tie. From his distinguished apparel, one would think that he was bred from money, but the diamond studs in his ear revealed his gangster, and his confident stature told a story of power. She could also see the imprint of a pistol on his hip.

*Yeah, you a hood nigga,* she thought as he approached her.

"This hardly seems fair. You know how to find me, but I can't even get a number to reach you," Britain said charmingly with a handsome smile as he took a seat across from her. His dark skin was flawless, and he had a slight scar above his right eye, but the imperfection only added to his appearance. His low-cut caesar was fresh, and his large brown eyes were magnetic as she matched his gaze.

"I don't want to become another notch on your belt. I'm not even going to set myself up to fall for you," Six replied, taking Britain by surprise.

"I'm not like that. Why don't you let me take you to dinner so you can find out," Britain stated.

"Dinner?" Six asked sarcastically.

"Yeah, you eat, don't you?" he stated with a laugh.

"Yeah, nigga, I eat. I've heard about you, though. I don't know if I'm trying to mess with somebody like you."

"See, you fucking up already. How are we supposed to build something together if you listening to what you hearing in the street?" Britain stated charismatically as he put his hand to his heart as if he was hurt by her quick judge of character.

"You saying what I've heard all on the news and all in the streets ain't true?" Six asked seriously as she looked at him across the table.

"Everything ain't what it seems, you know?"

"Yeah, I hear you," She responded skeptically. "So why are you so persistent on taking me out? I know you got these hoes going crazy out here."

"Because me and you we got history," Britain responded slyly.

"History?"

"You really don't remember me, huh?" he asked her.

"Am I supposed to?" Six asked as her arched eyebrows rose in confusion.

"I remember when you were walking around all bowlegged and snaggletoothed. You done filled out quite nicely, though."

"What are you talking about? I'm not even from here. I'm from—"

"New York . . . Bed-Stuy to be exact," Britain finished her sentence for her, causing her to put down her martini glass. She didn't know what type of games the nigga was playing, but she wasn't comfortable with him knowing her background, especially when she had not divulged the information to him herself.

"Don't look at me like I'm stalking you," Britain stated with a laugh. "Our pops used to run together back in the day. We used to play together when we were younger. You used to come to Detroit every summer to stay with him. You stopped coming when you were six years old."

"Oh my God!" she exclaimed, putting her hands over her mouth in disbelief as she recalled what he was saying. It had been so long, and he had changed so much that time had erased all memories of him. "I can't believe I didn't remember you," Six stated in disbelief.

"Don't worry about it—it was a long time ago. I remember you, though . . . vividly. You're not all knees and elbows anymore. You filled out quite nicely," he complimented.

She laughed and rolled her eyes at his blatant flirtation. "I was so rude to you. You talking about me filling out! I remember your little bean-head ass. You used to terrorize me."

"Only because I liked you." Britain smiled as he stared at Six.

"So this is all you?" Six asked as she looked around the popular downtown restaurant.

"Just a little business endeavor," he replied. "So can we go somewhere a bit more private?"

"I really shouldn't," Six replied. "I've heard a lot of fucked-up things about you," she admitted honestly.

"Six, I would never hurt you or put you in harm's way," Britain stated sincerely as he stood and held his hand out for her.

She relented and nodded her head before taking his hand and following him up the spiral stairs and into his office. It was modern with leather couches, a mahogany desk, and a flat-screen television. She was impressed as she looked around. His eyes followed her all over the room until she turned to catch him admiring her features.

"You staring at my ass like you've never seen one before," she commented and smiled.

He rubbed his goatee and motioned for her to sit down. She took a seat behind his desk and crossed her hands on top as if the place belonged to her.

"So what is all this that I hear about you? The streets got you pegged as a boss," Six stated.

"The streets just don't understand me. I'm not all bad, Six. I'm still that same kid you knew," Britain stated.

"That was a long time ago," she said in a low tone.

"Too long," Britain replied. "It's good seeing you again. Last time I checked you were fucking with that cat Free before he got locked up." Britain removed a bottle of champagne from the refrigerator and poured two flutes. He handed one to Six.

"So you were checking on me, huh?" she asked.

"I still fuck with your pops. That's where I saw you earlier this week. You were coming out of his house when I was pulling up. He had a picture of you and your dude," Britain explained. "You still in that situation?"

She shook her head. "No. He went to prison," she admitted.

"But he's out now," Britain replied quickly, letting her know that he was well-versed in all that was happening in the streets.

"How do you know all of this?" she questioned.

"I know everything that happens in my city."

"I don't fuck with him like that anymore. After he got out . . . things weren't the same. Too much time had passed and we were different. It didn't fit anymore," she explained.

Britain nodded in understanding and stared at her for so long that she avoided his gaze. He seemed to see straight through her.

"So dinner?" he asked again, charmingly persistent. Just the fact that he was showing so much interest flattered Six. She knew his reputation. Chicks all over the city were chasing him, and here he was pursuing her.

Six knew that a man like Britain was used to having his way, so she was going to make him work for everything, including her company. Courting her wouldn't be so easy for Britain.

"I don't know," she replied doubtfully. He walked around his desk and spun her chair around then bent over so that his face was inches from hers. Everything about him smelled good; he was so close to her that Six could smell the peppermint on his breath.

"I'm having a party at my beach house in Lake Fenton this weekend. I need a date. It's a group thing, so you won't feel uncomfortable, and you'll be safe. It will give me a chance to catch up with you some more. See where your head's at," he said.

She nodded and arose from his chair, but he made no effort to step back. They stood close to one another, neither of them uncomfortable with the lack of personal space. He swept a piece of hair out of her face.

"You really are beautiful, ma," he complimented. "You always have been."

She smiled. His words were so kind. . . . He was indeed a hood fella, but everything about his demeanor was so relaxed and composed. He had an edge of refinement that made him different than most dudes around the way. His twenty-five years on earth had done him well. He was attractive: A mix between businessman and thug, and with a twinge of conceit that made him irresistible. She grabbed a pen off her desk and wrote her number on the inside of his hand.

"I guess I will see you Saturday," she answered. She walked out of the office and down the stairs. Britain watched from the clear glass window in his office as she left the building, just as she knew he would. *I've got him,* she thought silently as she drove away.


"How did it go?" Free asked as soon as Six walked in the door.

"It went fine," she answered. "He invited me to his beach house this weekend."

Big Lou nodded and asked, "He's picking you up?"

"Probably so . . . but he can't scoop me from here," she said.

"You're going to have to move in with your pops for a few months . . . just tell him me and you are fighting. Don't let him know what's going on, though. You set that up and have Britain pick you up from there. Make him trust you, Six, but don't underestimate him. If you ever feel threatened you get out."

She nodded her head. She didn't want to tell Free that she and Britain knew each other back in the day. She figured it would only complicate the situation. "I will," she assured as she went into her bedroom to pack her bags. Her foot was in the door, now all she had to do was get the money and get out.

# Chapter Seven

Camera flashes and an onslaught of questions bombarded Britain as he walked out of the courtroom alongside his lawyers. Britain wore a neat mocha suit with gold cuff links to accessorize. His goons followed him closely as they trailed behind him, all wearing black Armani suits and designer shades. They were all scattered throughout the courtroom in support of their organization's leader. Britain had a superstar's arrogance and shook hands with his team of lawyers as he made his way toward the court's exit. He charismatically gave the reporters his boyish grin as he parted the massive crowd like Moses did the Red Sea.

The prosecutors were forced to postpone the trial because of the murder of their key witness. Without him they had no case. In Britain's mind, he knew that he was off the hook, but the murder of the federal agents comprised an entirely new dilemma.

His lead lawyer was a middle-aged Jewish man who had the charm of Johnnie Cochran. He pushed the microphones out of his client's face as he escorted him to his limo so that he could escape the pestering media. There were a line of limos in front of the courthouse that escorted his crew to and from the trial. His swagger was presidential.

Britain hid his drug money behind a string of Laundromats and seemed to be untouchable at that point. The DA hated it because of the irony behind it all. Britain owned the Laundromats to "wash" his dirty money. The district attorney shook his head in disgust as he watched the charade. It was as if Britain was thumbing his nose at the law and making a mockery of the Detroit Police Department. Britain gave one reporter a final wink before he approached his personal limo that was in front of the fleet.

"Okay, call me tomorrow. Congrats, Brick! We got this one in the bag," the lawyer whispered in his ear as he opened the limo door and watched as Britain got in.

"No doubt," Britain said as he sat in the vehicle and the lawyer closed his door shut. He took a deep breath as he rolled up his tinted window and leaned his head back in the headrest. "Turn that up," Britain instructed the driver as he heard the distant sound of legendary jazz musician Miles Davis on his radio. Feeling his phone vibrate on his hip, he signaled his limo driver to pull off as he pulled his phone off his belt-buckle clip. He smiled, seeing that it was Six texting him. It read:

I JUST SAW YOU ON THE NEWS. IT'S CRAZY HOW THE MOST WANTED MAN IN THE CITY OF DETROIT IS SO FASCINATED WITH ME. I MUST BE A LUCKY GIRL. LOOKING FORWARD TO SEEING YOU AGAIN. . . . SIX

Britain smiled as he put his phone back on his clip. He unbuckled his cuff links, loosened his tie, and popped a bottle of champagne that was waiting for him on ice in the back of the limo. "Feels good to be the boss," he whispered just before he took a gulp of the expensive drink. His limo pulled off and the fleet of limos followed.

Six opened her trunk and grabbed her luggage from the rear. "Daddy!" she yelled, needing his help. Jones immediately emerged from the house with a joint hanging from his lip and a straw hat on. "Hold on, baby. I got you," he said as he hurried, while still walking smoothly. Jones grabbed the big luggage from Six and pulled it out of the trunk for her.

"Thanks, Daddy," she said as she grabbed her smaller Gucci bags from the backseat.

"No problem," Jones said as he carried the luggage in the house.

"Thanks for letting me stay here with you for a while," Six said as she followed her father into his house.

"No problem, baby. It will feel like old times when you used to love ya' old man," Jones said smiling, slightly out of breath, and set the luggage down on the floor. Then he sat down on the couch and lit his joint. Six put her bags down and sat next to him.

"Daddy, you know I love you," she said, smiling back. Jones took a deep pull and handed her the joint. Six took the joint in between her index and pointing fingers and placed it to her lips. She inhaled deeply and knew that she was smoking nothing but the best. Jones always had the grade-A, top-shelf smoke.

"What's going on with you and Free?" he asked, knowing something was up because Six had asked him if could she stay with him for a while.

"Nothing that I can't handle, Daddy," she said as she passed the weed back to him. "We have just been arguing so damn much and need some space."

"Well, you guys are going to get it together. Free is a good nigga. Little rough around the edges, but I can tell he really loves you," Jones said as he pointed his finger at Six knowingly. "If you're anything like your mama, you got a mouth on you. You probably be nagging him to death."

"Yeah, yeah . . . don't nobody be bothering that boy and I don't nag. We are going to be good, though. Just need some space," Six responded, not wanting to let her father know about the plan to rob Britain, knowing he would disapprove. She felt bad for lying to her father, even if it was small. She had never had to lie to him, and their relationship was built on trust. However, Six knew it was best for Jones not to know about the plan. She knew how close Brick's father and Jones were back in the day and she also knew there, was deep loyalty between the two families and she was breaking that. *Fuck it! I got to hold my man down no matter what,* she thought. Free had asked her to do it, and she was going to come through for him no matter what.

Jones nodded while remaining secretly suspicious. He knew how close Six and Free were, and it didn't add up to him. A father's intuition let him know that something was going on. He smiled and took a deep drag of his doobie, letting the smoke rest in his lungs before he blew it back out in circles. Nevertheless, he was glad to have Six around, so he wasn't complaining. "Glad to have to you home, baby girl," he said giving her his famous smile.

# Chapter Eight

Six sat on the porch with her father and he passed her the joint he was blazing. She hit it, held the smoke in her lungs, and passed it back to him. She loved her daddy. He had always been there for her. When her mother moved to New York, it broke Six's heart, because she couldn't see her father every day. When she was younger, she always looked forward to visiting him each summer.

He had done everything to provide her with the life of a princess. He also kept it real and schooled Six about the streets. He never wanted a man to be able to game his baby girl, so he taught her to be savvy in the ways of the world and to always stay two steps ahead of everyone else. They had always been closer than close because he treated her with respect and vice versa. When he first caught her smoking weed, he didn't get mad, he taught her how to roll her own blunt so that someone in the streets couldn't slip her anything. When she tasted her first sip of liquor, it was he who gave it to her. He got her so fucked up that she never drank herself to the point of intoxication again. When he found out she was having sex, however, he beat her ass until no tomorrow . . . then sat down and told her not to spread her legs for just any man. He taught her self-respect and told her to make a man earn everything she gave him, including her heart. It was for these reasons that she loved her father dearly. It was not the conventional father-daughter relationship, but it was a bond that no one could break.

"You sure Free don't mind you going out with Britain?" Jones asked, protecting the interests of Free.

Six laughed at her overprotective father and replied, "Daddy, Free knows Britain and I are just friends. Don't worry about it. Besides, I thought you liked Britain."

Jones nodded as he blew smoke into the air. "I do like the li'l mu'fucka. I just know if he's anything like his father then the nigga ain't easy on no bitch. His old man used to love 'em and leave 'em," he said.

Six shook her head in amazement at her father. "Daddy, you a trip. You was right there with his father, probably gaming up all the chicks back in the day," she accused playfully.

"You damn right," Jones replied proudly as he inhaled the weed smoke like a pro.

Their conversation was interrupted by the sound of music coming down the street. Britain pulled in front of the house with a Silver Range Rover and was pulling a medium-sized luxury boat on a trailer behind him. Six smiled and approached him as he got out of the car.

The khaki Ralph Lauren cargo shorts and white polo he wore impressed her, and she wrapped her arms around him as he embraced her for a hug. He picked her up from the ground a little when he hugged her.

"You look nice," he said in her ear, causing her to blush. There was something about his compliments that made her feel like a schoolgirl. She didn't know if it was his deep baritone or the way he whispered it as if only her ears were worthy of hearing the truth.

"What's good, Jones?" he greeted as he slapped hands with her father.

"You, son . . . you," Jones said as he snuffed out the joint and grabbed Six's bag. He stepped off the porch and handed her things to Britain. "You take care of her."

"No doubt, Jones. Don't worry. I'm not another nigga. I know how you get down, and you know how I get down, because you taught me. She's in safe hands," Britain assured.

"Bye, Daddy," Six said as she stood on her tip-toes and kissed his cheek.

"Hmm," he grunted. Just his demeanor let her know that he didn't like the fact that she was going out with Britain. He was on Team Free, and he didn't know exactly what was going on yet, but he knew that something wasn't quite right. Although Free's paper wasn't right, Jones loved Free's heart. He knew that Free was a real nigga, and that's all a father could ask of the man that wifed his daughter.

Britain put his hand on the small of her back and opened her car door, then jogged around to the driver's side and pulled off, hitting his horn twice to say good-bye to Jones.

"I'm sorry. You know how he is," Six stated.

"Yeah, I know," Britain replied with a smile. He reached over to grab her hand and she let him. She noticed that he was the type of dude who didn't mind showing his interest, so she made sure to reciprocate his actions. *I don't want him to think I'm not interested,* she thought. He put in a mix tape, and they rode in comfortable silence until they arrived at their destination.

"You ready to smile for the cameras, ma?" he asked.

"What are you talking about?" she replied. "What cameras?"

As soon as the words left her mouth, Britain turned onto the road where his beach house was located. News vans and camera crews crowded the streets, and reporters rushed his way as he maneuvered into the driveway.

"What are they here for?" she asked.

"This case is keeping my face in the news," he informed her. "Don't answer any questions. I'm going to come around to your side of the car and get you."

"This is crazy," she said as she looked around at the mayhem outside.

Britain exited his vehicle and was swarmed with questions as he went to open Six's door. He pulled her gently from the car and she tucked her head into his chest as he made his way through the media.

"Britain, who is the young lady?"

"Does she know you're a murderer?"

"Did you have anything to do with the killings of the key witness and the federal officers?"

The questions came one after another until they were safely inside of his lakeside house.

"How do you live like that?" she asked.

"Once they find something new to talk about, the press will die down. I've been under a microscope twenty-four hours a day since my trial began. If it isn't the police, it is the media. I don't call that living, but today, you blessed me with your presence . . . that makes today better than yesterday. I just hope you'll give me a chance so that you will be here to help me make tomorrow better than today," he said.

Six couldn't help the grin that spread on her face as she shook her head as if she didn't believe him. She pointed her finger at him and frowned. "Don't be gaming me, Britain. Nigga, I know bullshit when I hear it."

"Nah, that's real, Six," he stated as he kissed the back of her hand. "Let me introduce you to everyone."

Britain escorted Six to the backyard and made his rounds with her on his arm. Everyone showed her love just off the strength that she was his guest of honor. They all knew that he was feeling her because usually their hood affairs were for insiders only. The fact that he had even asked her to come was a big deal.

Tables were set up in the shape of a rectangle, and Britain took his seat at the head and positioned her by his side. They all stood to bless the food, and then they ate like royalty. Waiters in white coats came and tended to Six's every need.

"Do you do everything so extravagant?" she asked.

"It's the only way to do it, ma. You only live life once. I can't take my paper with me when I die," he said. "Enjoy yourself. Whatever you need, just let me know, and I'll make it happen for you."

One of his henchmen stood and raised his glass, which signaled everyone else to follow suit.

"I'm toasting this one out to B. Bricks," the dude said, referring to Britain by his nickname. "They tried to knock my man off his throne, but it didn't work. A case like that is nothing to a giant. We're glad you're home, fam. Fuck the feds!" the man said as he raised his glass.

"Fuck the feds!" everyone yelled and clapped. Britain raised his glass graciously and nodded in salute to his loyal team of workers. They had all come up in the street together, and Six could feel the love and loyalty among the group. They were like a family, and she was so caught up in the moment that she leaned over and whispered, "You really are a king."

He grabbed her chin and kissed her lips. Her body tensed. She hadn't kissed another man besides Free in so long that it didn't even feel right. Extreme guilt plagued her. She felt like a cheat, even though it was Free himself who had urged her to do this. She knew that it was important for her to play the role, so she pushed Free out of her mind and focused on the gentleman in front of her. She kissed Britain back, their tongues doing a delicate dance. He grabbed her neck gently. His touch was so affectionate that she felt like she was really his girl . . . if only for this moment.

"Today you're the queen of the streets," he replied as he pulled away. She beamed and played her position the rest of the day. It wasn't hard to do . . . Britain made it simple to be his lady. He catered to her all day. Even though there were a hundred people at the celebration, he only had time for her. They popped bottles of champagne on the sandy beach until the wee hours of the morning. By three A.M. the party had died down. The only person who remained was Britain's right-hand man.

"Yo, B, I need to rap business with you before I jet," he said.

Britain motioned for the guy to take a seat as he put his glass of liquor on the table. "Don't take up too much of my time. My attention is elsewhere, nah'mean?" he said as he stared Six in the eyes.

"No disrespect, Brick, but I definitely know what you mean, fam. Who can talk business with someone so distracting in the room," the goon stated as he took a quick peek at Six.

Six blushed, and Britain pointed a warning finger and replied, "Stay in your lane, my nigga. What's good on this business?"

The dude rubbed his hands together and adjusted his Yankee fitted on his head .

"That shipment is supposed to be here Monday night. They're going to meet us at the old Ford factory off I-94 at midnight," the guy said.

Six turned her head to pretend as if she weren't interested in what was going on, but she was ear hustling as she made mental notes of all the details.

"Okay, make sure that it is picked up on time and test my work before you make the exchange. That's a hundred grand you playing with. . . . Make sure it's done right," Britain replied.

Six's heartbeat sped up as she eavesdropped on the conversation. *A hundred thou is a lot of money. We need that,* she thought. Free's face flashed in her mind. She opened her purse as Britain walked his goon to the door. Quickly, he retrieved her cell phone to text Free.

"Fuck," she whispered when she discovered that she didn't have service.

When Britain returned, Six was more than eager to get home. "Don't you think we should head back to Detroit?" she asked. All of a sudden she was anxious to get back to her man. She could not wait to tell him about the shipment.

"We're staying the weekend here," Britain replied.

"The weekend?" she exclaimed. "I didn't even bring a change of clothes. I only have my swimsuit and what I'm wearing today."

"Then I guess we will have to raid a mall tomorrow morning," he said with a smile. He could see by the look on her face that she wasn't happy. He pulled her close. "If you really want to go back to Detroit tonight, I'll take you, but I would prefer if you would stay."

She rolled her eyes and nodded her head, giving in to him. There was something about the way he spoke to her that made it hard for her to say no. She determined right then that she would have to be careful around him. If she was not careful, he would penetrate her heart. She had to make sure that she stayed focused.

"Can I at least get a T-shirt or something so that I can shower?" she asked with an attitude.

He led her upstairs and handed her a towel and a shirt then left the room.

Six checked her phone for service one last time and sighed in frustration. She turned it off for the night, showered, then returned downstairs. Even the white T-shirt looked like designer threads on her. It hugged her curves when she walked, giving Britain a good idea of what she was barely hiding underneath.

"Remember when we were kids you told me that yellow snow was where lemon-flavored ices came from?" he asked as he motioned for her to sit down.

Six burst into laughter and held her stomach tightly as she recalled him eating the pissy snow.

"You were such a sucker," she said as tears came to her eyes while she continued to chuckle.

Britain shook his head in embarrassment. "I trusted anything you told me back then. I thought you were the flyest six-year-old on the block."

"That's because I was," Six replied with conceit.

"And now?"

"Now what?" she asked.

"You still out here making cats eat yellow piss?" he asked.

"In other words, you're asking me can you trust me?" she answered.

"Well, can I?"

*You shouldn't,* she answered in her head, feeling guilty that she was playing him the way she was, but aloud, she replied, "Yes, Britain. I'm a grown woman now, and I don't have time for games. If I choose you, I will always be loyal to you."

It was not really a lie. Six had not chosen to be with Britain. Her heart belonged to Free, and although he was asking her to do something as extreme as this, she was riding for him until the end. She chose Free, and unfortunately for Britain, he had crossed Free, which meant that he had inadvertently crossed Six as well.

"What do I have to do to get you to choose me?" he asked seriously.

Six shrugged. "I don't know. We'll take it day by day and see where this leads," she said. "Since you have me trapped up here for the entire weekend, what do you have planned?" she asked.

"I'm going to take you out on my boat tomorrow," he said as he stood. He kissed her forehead then started out of the room. "You can take the master bedroom upstairs. I'll sleep in the guest room. Get some sleep. We're waking up early tomorrow to go out on the lake," he informed her, just before leaving the room.

The smell of food burning awoke Six out of her sleep. She looked over at the clock and noticed that it was five in the morning. The sun hadn't even come up yet. She pulled back the covers and crawled out of bed. The thousand-thread sheets urged her to lie back down, but she forced herself to get up.

"Britain!" she called out as she stepped into a hallway full of smoke. The smoke alarm was going off, and she heard him moving around downstairs. She made her way down the stairs and stepped into the gourmet kitchen, where she put her hand over her mouth as she watched Britain scrambling around the room in an attempt to cook breakfast.

"Boy, what are you doing?" she asked.

"Sit down, breakfast will be done in a minute," he said as he reached for a skillet on the stove.

Six reached out her hand to stop him. "Britain, you might wanna—"

"Agh, fuck!" he exclaimed as he grabbed the hot handle before she could get a chance to warn him.

"Okay here, sit down," she said as she pulled out a chair for him. She cut down the fire on the stove and then retrieved some ice out of the freezer. Kneeling in front of him she grabbed his hand while shaking her head then applied the ice to his burn. "Why are you up so early making breakfast?" she asked as she nursed his aching hand.

"Don't women like that breakfast-in-bed bull-shit?" he asked.

"You were cooking for me?" she asked in surprise. Six reached up and put her hands behind his head to pull him near. She kissed his lips quickly and then hopped to her feet. "That was sweet, but what do you have me here for if you're not going to use me? You let me handle breakfast."

Britain watched as Six moved around the kitchen like a master chef. She was so feminine, but so hood at the same time. He could see himself building something great with her one day. He eased up behind her as she cooked and wrapped his hands around her waist. He felt her body tense. It was something that he noticed every time he got too close.

Six's breath caught in her throat. Free hadn't prepared her for these intimate moments. She hadn't expected to have butterflies or feel jittery around Britain. The way her body responded to him surprised even her.

"Are you afraid of me?" he asked as he kissed the back of her neck, causing her eyes to close as she imagined his full lips exploring other parts of her body.

She maneuvered out of his touch. His hands were not Free's hands. She had to remember that. She couldn't allow herself to get in too deep.

"I'm afraid of what I'm getting myself into," she replied honestly.

"I would never bring you into my world if I didn't think you belonged, Six. You don't have to be uncomfortable around me, and I don't want you to fear me, ma. Everything you've heard in the streets isn't really who I am. That's how I handle business. This with you isn't business."

"I'm not uncomfortable around you, Britain. I'm too comfortable," she whispered. She fixed two plates and set them on the kitchen table.

"That's a bad thing?" he asked as he took her hands in his.

She sighed as she looked up at the man who used to be her childhood friend. She felt horrible for what she was setting him up for, but she had to remind herself that Britain deserved what he had coming to him. He had stiffed Free, and money out of Free's pocket was jeopardizing Six's life. If she didn't put her conscience to the side, then the Russians would kill her. She didn't have a choice.

*I have to do this,* she thought. *It's either him or me.*

"It's not a bad thing at all," she finally replied.

The two sat down to breakfast, and Six decided to go all in. It was the only way that she was going to get to the money. She couldn't half step. She had to handle her end of the setup so that Britain would give her access to his safe.

# Chapter Nine

"You say it's going to be a hundred-thousand-dollar deal?" Free asked, not believing his ears.

"Yeah, that's what he said," Six confirmed as she sat on her bed and talked to Free who was pacing the small room in Jones's house. She tried to whisper, because Jones was only one room away in his bedroom

"Good. Good. I'ma hit his ass. He will never see it coming," Free said smiling and rubbing his hands together as he began plotting in his mind. "What else did he say?" Free asked as he sat next to Six on the bed.

"He didn't say too much. Just that the drop-off was sometime tonight at the old Ford factory off of I-94."

"I'ma have to get there early and camp out. I got to call Lou and . . ." Free stopped in his tracks as Jones peeked in.

"Hey, Daddy," Six said as she smiled, wondering if he overheard her talking about robbing

Britain. Jones remained silent as he smiled and shook his head from side to side.

"I couldn't help but overhear y'all conversation," Jones said as he walked in with his smooth stroll. He slipped his hand in his shirt's top pocket, pulled out a pack of Newport cigarettes, and began to smack the bottom of the box. "If y'all fall for that trick, y'all both some damn fools. That's the oldest trick in the book," he said as he pulled out a cigarette and lit it.

"What you talking about?" Six asked.

"Meeting Britain at that Ford factory is a setup. To test you, Six. Now let me ask you a question. Did he talk about the exchange right in front of you?" Jones asked.

"Yeah," Six admitted, not wanting to lie to her father.

"See, that was his bait for you. He wants to test your loyalty. I taught him that trick years ago," Jones said as he smiled, thinking about how he used to pull that trick on women back in the day.

"He might be right," Free agreed as he began to rub the hair that was on his chin. "Can't see how I missed that one," he said as he nodded in agreement.

"Not trying to be in y'all business, but if you gonna do it . . . do it right. Britain is a smart man, and this is chess, not checkers, youngblood,"

Jones said to Free as if he was subliminally saying something else. Jones gave him a look that said, "Take care of my daughter and don't have her going into situations ass backward." He then walked out of the room blowing smoke into the air, leaving them thinking about what he said. Needless to say, Free and Lou never made it to the drop-off that night.


Britain and his goon waited patiently in his car, parked discreetly under the highway's overpass. The car was positioned so he had a clear view of the old factory. He was hoping that Free didn't show up just because he could see himself starting something serious with Six.

"You think she sent ol' boy?" the goon asked as he sat in the driver's seat next to Britain.

"Don't know. I can't read her, for some reason," Britain said as he looked on attentively, waiting for someone to come.

He was an overly cautious man and he couldn't afford to let anyone into his circle who was a potential enemy. Some people would call staking out a fake exchange ridiculous, but Britain called it being smart. He looked down at his watch. Almost two A.M. So far no sign of her treachery had occurred. Nobody had even driven past the old factory. He smiled as he texted Six.

GOOD NIGHT, I'M GOING TO BED. HOPE
YOU HAVE A GOOD SLEEP.
    BRICK

"Let's get out of here," Britain directed his
goon as he smiled and threw his head back in his
headrest. He was ready to show Six how much
he was into her. Little did he know that she was
potentially his downfall.


"Ooh," Six crooned, slowly moving her hips
in circular motions as she thrust her pelvis into
Free's face. She rode him in a slow rhythm. Her
juice box was directly on his mouth as he moved
his tongue like a tornado, giving Six ecstasy. She
was grateful that her father had an outing with
one of his pretty young things and left her the
house alone with Free. She hadn't felt him inside
of her in a while and she was long overdue for his
love. She hopped off his face and straddled his
bottom half. Free slid straight into her and the
sounds of her gushing wetness echoed throughout the room. She took him all in as her ass met
his testicles.

"Oh God," she said as she felt his rockhard pole
filling her up. She instantly had an orgasm, squirt-

ing lightly on his stomach as she grinded against him, all while he rubbed her clitoris. "Right there," she said as she sped up her pace and gripped his toned chest. Free then palmed her cheeks and gently smacked her left butt cheek, giving her a light sting.

"Damn, baby. You riding that," he moaned as she rode his body like a snake. She closed her eyes and began to rub on her own breasts, stimulating her erect nipples.

"Br—" Six caught herself as she was about to call Free Britain's name. Her eyes shot wide open, hoping that Free did catch her slipup. Free's eyes were closed, and he grinded from the bottom, so she knew that he hadn't heard her. *Oh shit*, she thought as she hopped off him and turned around so he could enter her from the back. She couldn't stand to look at him in the face. She felt so guilty. She buried her head in the pillow, and Free entered her, slowly rocking in and out, giving her pleasure with every strategic stroke.

Free gave Six the business that night and made her climax plenty of times. Instead of walking into a trap at the old Ford factory, Free was making love to his favorite woman in the world. Little did he know, her mind was on the man that she was supposed to be deceiving . . . Britain.

# Chapter Ten

It felt weird staying with her father again. She hadn't spent the night in his home in a very long time, but she was glad that she was back so that they could spend some quality time together. As the sun crept through her blinds, Six sat up and stretched her arms out. She had gotten a perfect night's sleep. There was something about being underneath her father's roof that made her feel safe. She felt untouchable because she knew that her daddy would never let anything happen to her.

*I'ma make him something to eat,* she thought as she stepped into her house shoes and walked out of the room and into the kitchen. As soon as she entered the kitchen, she saw a note from her father on the counter.

*Morning, baby girl, I'm out fishing. Won't be back soon. I left you some pocket change on the counter and your favorite cereal is in the cabinet.*

*I love you always,*
*Daddy*

Six looked at the hundred-dollar bill that was on the countertop and shook her head while smiling. *He still treats me like his baby,* she thought as she went to the cabinet to retrieve the box of cinnamon toast crunch that her father knew she loved.

She sat down in the living room with her cereal in hand and curled up on the couch. Then she picked up her cell phone to call Free.

*Ding-dong!*

Six ended the call abruptly when she heard the doorbell ring. Opening the door, she was greeted by a white woman in a cream-colored suit. Six recognized the designer Dolce threads immediately. Her eyebrows creased as she wondered what the upscale woman was doing on her father's doorstep.

"Can I help you?" Six asked.

"My name is Melissa Warren. I have a letter for a Ms. Six Jones," the jeweler stated.

Six leaned against the frame of the door and replied, "That's me . . . a letter from who?"

The woman gave her a bright smile and handed over a chocolate brown-and-gold envelope. Six opened the letter in suspense, anxious to see what was going on.

*Today I show you what it's like to fuck with a boss. Today is your day, ma. A limo is going to pick you up in one hour and take you to Somerset mall. You can have whatever you like. Just have the cashiers put your purchases on my account. Enjoy yourself and don't hurt me too bad. The limo will bring you back to my place later tonight. I have something special planned. I'll see you then.*

  *Britain*

Six was cheesing from ear to ear by the time she was done reading the letter and when she looked up, she gasped in surprise.

The woman was standing in front of her with a briefcase full of diamond jewelry. "He must really love you to buy such an expensive gift," the woman stated. "You can pick any piece you like."

Six's chin dropped to her chest as she stepped to the side and let the woman in. "Oh my God," she whispered. Britain was pulling out all stops, and the extravagance of it all floored her. She was like a kid in a candy store as she sat down across from the woman and began to try on the expensive jewels.

"This here is a Harry Winston piece. It's a two-karat diamond ring," the woman said, going on to describe the cut of the ring as she placed it on Six's finger. Six held out her hand and looked at the rock as she imagined what her wedding ring would look like someday. She shook her head and removed it from her finger.

"It's too much like an engagement ring," she said as she placed it back into the lady's hands. She leaned over the coffee table where every piece was spread out on top of a velvet cloth. "What about that?" she asked pointing to a necklace.

"You have great taste," the woman stated as she grabbed the necklace and walked behind Six to put it on for her. "This is a Tiffany's piece. Platinum rope with a ten-karat colorless diamond." She fastened it around Six's neck. "Wow! That is beautiful on you. The size of it overwhelms most women, but it fits you perfectly."

Six walked over to the wall mirror and gasped when she saw the diamond resting against her neck. She touched it as if it couldn't be real. She had never seen anything so beautiful. "How much is it?" she asked.

"Twenty-seven thousand dollars," the woman answered.

Six shook her head. "I can't choose this. That's way too much," she said.

"Mr. Adams instructed me to bring only the best. I think he'll be pleased with your selection. Just between you and me . . . your limit was seventy-five thousand dollars," she said, whispering the last part.

Six fingered the necklace and took a deep breath, a bit overwhelmed by Britain's bottomless wallet. "Okay, I'll take it," she said, smiling.

"Wonderful selection. It was nice meeting you, Six. I'm Mr. Adams's personal jeweler. I'll probably be seeing you again," she said as she extended her hand.

Six shook it and replied, "Nice meeting you too."

Dressing quickly, Six put on a cocoa-colored, floor-length maxi dress and sandals while pulling her hair off her face in a ponytail. She wanted to be as relaxed as possible because she knew that she was in for a day of pampering . . . courtesy of Britain. He was flattering her to no end, pulling out all stops in order to win her favor. She knew that he had probably charmed many women in his day, but she couldn't help but feel special. He showered her with attention. Even though they had not seen each other since they were very young, somehow he always knew the right things to say and do to get her loose. Every time she shut her emotions down and blocked him out, he did something new to win her over. She was beginning to think he had done this before with many women, because he was too good at playing the gentleman role.

Just as she applied the last of her M•A•C cosmetics the doorbell rang again, announcing the arrival of her limo. At that exact moment, Free called her phone. She sighed as she stared at his name as it flashed across the screen of her cell. She loved Free, but his constant presence made it harder for her to get the job done. *He's gonna have to give me a little space,* she thought. *That's not asking too much.*

Six picked up her purse and put on her Christian Dior shades and walked out the door, hitting the ignore button to stop the call. She sent Free to voice mail. She didn't want to hear his voice right now. He would only remind her that her relationship with Britain wasn't real, and at that moment, she could not bear to hear it, even if it was the truth.

# Chapter Eleven

Six stared out the window of the limo as she was escorted to the east side of the city.

"Where are we going?" she asked.

"I was instructed not to answer any questions. I don't want to ruin the surprise," the driver responded.

Six sat back in her seat and rolled up the window to separate herself from the driver. She had no clue what Britain had up his sleeve, but there was not a doubt in her mind that she would enjoy it. He had given her a beautiful day, allowing her to dine, shop, and experience the luxuries of being a dopeman's wife. She felt rejuvenated. From her pedicured French-tip toes to her freshly dyed and layered hair, she shined.

She took a deep breath as the limo pulled into the luxury community of Grosse Pointe Woods. Looking around at all of the million-dollar houses, her mouth opened in shock. *I know he don't own nothing out here,* she thought. She knew that Britain was major, but to have a house in Gross Pointe Woods, he had to moving weight like Escobar. She had really been sleeping on Britain's status.

She quickly pulled out her foundation compact and checked to make sure her makeup was on point. Everything was perfect. She looked like a true diva in her brand-new Marciano one-shoulder cocktail dress, but despite the physical transformation her insecurities surfaced as butterflies danced in her stomach while she was being transported to destination unknown. Finally, they pulled into a long driveway and onto the grounds of one of the homes. Six's wide eyes took everything in. From the opulent garden, to the luxurious fountain, and the well-maintained yards . . . everything around her spelled M-o-n-e-y. It was the most amazing house she had ever laid eyes on.

The minimansion was magnificent and it took her breath away, making her feel as if she didn't belong. She was just a girl from the ghetto . . . born on the north side of Detroit and raised in New York City. How she had even gotten to be in someone's company who could afford something so great was beyond her.

She could see Britain standing at the top of his steps waiting for her to exit the limo. He was clean in gray Ferragamo slacks and a black and gray sweater. She smiled because he was far from the square he dressed like. He was so gangster and powerful, just thinking about his reign over the streets made her wet. Her palms began to sweat. The closer the car got to Britain, the more nervous she became.

It seemed like a lifetime passed by before the car finally reached him. White rose petals were situated on both sides of the entryway, making an aisle that led directly to Britain. She reached to open the door, but halted when she heard her phone ring.

"Fuck!" she whispered to herself when she realized that it was Free trying to reach her. She held the phone tightly in her hand and began to answer it when Britain knocked on the limo window. She hit the ignore button and turned off her phone, then stuck it in her handbag. *I'll call him later*, she thought.

She unlocked the door for Britain. He opened it, and then extended his hand to help her out. "You look beautiful, ma," he stated with a grin.

"What are you smiling for?" she asked. "I look stupid in this . . . it's too fancy, right?" She nervously rubbed her hands on her dress as she clutched her bag tightly.

"Nah, you look perfect. Got to retire them skinny jeans . . . too many niggas can see what's mine when you rock 'em," he stated only half jokingly.

"What's yours, huh?" she rebutted.

He nodded conceitedly and grabbed her hand to take her into his home. As soon as she stepped foot inside, she couldn't believe her eyes.

"You live here?" she asked, knowing that she sounded like a naïve girl who had never been anywhere or had seen anything, but the truth was Britain had her on some new shit. Even Free hadn't exposed her to this quality of life. Britain was living the high life. . . . Niggas rapped about his reality in their songs and here it was within her arm's reach.

He chuckled and nodded as he swept his hands around. "Yeah, this is my home."

"It's nice," she said as she looked around. "You live here by yourself?" she asked.

He nodded. "Until I can find someone to share it with, yes . . . it's just me."

"Your shit is so plush," she stated in amazement. "You want to give me a tour?" she asked.

Britain held up his finger and left the room only to reenter moments later with a bottle of Dom Pérignon in his hand. He grabbed two champagne flutes that were on the table and poured them each a drink. "Now I can show you around," he stated as he began to walk up the glass staircase.

Six's stilettos clicked on the stairs and when she looked down, she noticed that each stair had a different exotic fish swimming behind the glass. She smiled. "This is so unreal," she whispered, highly pleased with her surroundings.

He took her from room to room, and she loved every minute of it. She made him show her his entire house, including his theater room and inside basketball court. It took them an hour to view everything, and when he was done she shook her head at a loss for words.

"I take it you like it?" he asked.

"Boy, are you kidding? I love it!" she exclaimed as she finished her second glass of champagne. She was so enthralled with it all that she couldn't sit still. She walked along his entryway and looked at the pictures on the wall. One in particular stopped her dead in her tracks. She stared at a picture of herself when she was little. She was standing in between Britain and his father; they were all holding a huge fish together. Her hand covered her mouth in surprise as she remembered that day. It had been so long ago that she had erased it from her memory bank. She turned back to Britain.

"My father took this picture of us, didn't he?" she asked.

He pointed his pinkie toward the picture while holding his champagne glass and replied, "Yeah . . . you remember that?" he asked.

She nodded and turned back to the picture. She looked so young . . . so innocent. It was a shame what the world had turned her into. She was a con artist. A manipulative and untrustworthy woman. She barely even recognized the youthful face smiling at her from behind the frame.

"That's how I recognized you when I saw you at your father's crib. I've been looking at your face every day for the past fifteen years. It's the only picture that I have of my pops, so I cherish it. As soon as I saw you again, I knew who you were," Britain explained. "I could never forget your face."

She teared up as she listened to his story. "How did he die?"

He walked up behind her and stood so close that she could feel the imprint of his manhood brush her behind through the thin fabric of her dress.

"He was killed. A man he robbed came back and shot him right in front of me," Britain stated.

She turned to face him. "I'm sorry," she said sincerely. "I remember your father. He was a good man."

Britain shook his head in objection. "Nah, he was a good father and a good friend to Jones. My pops was a goon. . . . He played the game and lost. His one mistake was letting the nigga that he robbed live. When you're doing dirt, you don't leave loose ends. He robbed a man and let him live . . . that one decision cost him his life."

As Britain spoke, Six thought about what she was doing. Essentially, she was doing the same thing. This entire game with Britain was nothing more than a huge setup to rob him.

*Will he come for me after he finds out what I did? Is he going to kill me like that man did his father?* she thought.

"What happened to the man who killed your father?" she asked.

"I killed his wife and kids," he stated coldly while staring at the picture of his father as if in a trance. He had never told anyone that he had committed those murders, but he felt at ease with Six.

Six stepped back from him as she observed the calculating look in his eyes. The cat had her tongue, and the hairs on the back of her neck stood up. She had underestimated Britain. She was quickly realizing that she had no idea what he was capable of.

"He took something from me, and I took something from him. An eye for an eye," Britain stated. He glanced down at her and noticed that she was trembling. He put his hand on her neck and massaged it as he traced her jawline with one finger. "I told you not to fear me, ma. I would never hurt you. I don't let too many know where I rest my head, but I know that I can trust you. You've already passed my test."

Six didn't respond so he continued. "I knew that you used to fuck with a stickup nigga. Free used to put in work back in the day so I couldn't be caught slipping. When we were up north at my beach house, I purposefully put some information out about one of my pickups. I knew that you could hear me, so I wanted to see what you would do with that info. I went to the spot and waited for the nigga Free to show up. If he came, I would have known that you sent him. . . . But he didn't come, so now I know that you don't have loose lips."

"I told you I don't deal with Free like that anymore," she stated.

"I had to be sure. You don't get where I am by making mistakes. . . . Everyone around me has a test to pass before I let them in. You passed it, and you're in," he replied.

"Good to know," she smiled as she raised her glass, and he poured more champagne inside.

She was grateful for the drink and downed it in one huge gulp. She needed it to calm her nerves.

"You want something a little bit stronger?" Britain asked with a laugh.

"Actually I do . . . forget all this champagne. Pull out the liquor," Six stated. "I'ma show you how I used to do it in Brooklyn."

"Nah, ma, I'ma show you how I do it everywhere," Britain replied arrogantly as he walked to the bar that decorated the corner of the room and plucked a bottle of Patrón from his shelf. "You off this with me?"

Six nodded, her eyes low and mischievous from the glasses of champagne she had consumed. She took a seat at one of the stools.

He pulled out two shot glasses and filled them both to the rim.

"You got salt and lime?" she asked.

He nodded toward the kitchen and then admired the sway of her wide hips as she went to retrieve the items.

When she returned, he held up the glass for her. "You ready?" he asked.

"Nigga, you ready?" she countered playfully. She placed the salt on her hand and licked it off seductively. Then she chased it with the liquor and then the lime. As the top-shelf tequila went down her throat, burning her vocals on the way down she cringed and said "Aghh!" then stuck out her tongue afterward. "Your turn," she demanded as she put more salt on her hand and held it out for Britain to lick. "Come on, Britain," she urged. "Time to turn the good-guy act off. . . . Introduce me to Brick. I want to see what the streets see."

Britain took her hand and licked the salt off, slowly tonguing between all of her fingers, making Six's breathing become heavy, lustful. His tongue was so juicy and thick that it made Six cream in her panties. She pulled her hand away and shook it as if he had set it ablaze, when in actuality, he had set her clitoris on fire.

Britain laughed arrogantly and hit the shot while keeping his eyes on Six. She placed the lime in his mouth, and he bit it until the juice flowed down her wrist. Then he took her hand in his and kissed the back of her wrist. The feeling of his lips on her skin made her eyes close against her will.

"Britain," she whispered.

"What up, ma?" he responded as he bit his bottom lip and leaned across the bar so that they were face-to-face.

"There's so much you don't know about me," she stated as tears came to her eyes.

"I know all that I need to know, Six," Britain responded. He kissed her lips, and she turned her head to the side to kiss him back. At that instant she blocked the rest of the world out. She didn't want to think about the moment, because she knew if she contemplated her actions she would stop herself. She just wanted to let it happen. Britain made her feel special . . . loved . . . unique. *He's nothing like Free,* she thought as her tongue tasted the tequila that Britain had consumed.

"Wait," she said as she pulled back.

Britain wiped his mouth with his fingers and nodded.

"I'm sorry," she said. "I'm just—my head is all over the place when it comes to you. I don't think I'm ready."

"It's okay, Six. I respect you. I'll wait as long as you need me to," Britain stated as he raised the bottle of Patrón to his lips and hit a shot straight from the bottle.

Six chuckled as she noticed how hot and bothered she had made Britain. She reached for the bottle because he had her the same way. "I need some of that too," she stated with laughter in her voice. She took it to the head and continued to laugh as they passed the bottle back and forth.

"You're gonna kill me, ma," he stated. "Got my blood pressure up and shit," he joked as they sat at the bar getting drunk together.

"Trust me . . . it's worth the wait," she responded seductively while raising her eyebrows.

"Quit playing with me," he said as he chased her around the bar.

"It's so good . . . I promise you," she laughed while being chased around the great room. It reminded her of when they were kids. She stopped running so that she could take another hit of the bottle that was still in her hand. Britain picked her up and spun her around, then dropped her on the cushiony French sofa.

"I'ma fuck you up," he stated playfully as they both laughed together.

It was then that Six realized that she had missed their friendship. She remembered the innocent trust that they used to have in one another all of those years ago. It was childish and insignificant at the time, but it had been the purest friendship that Six had ever had. It was before she knew anything about hitting licks or coping with life's everyday grind. She was sure that in another lifetime Britain would be her man. A part of her was sad that true love could never be in the cards for them. *He's so perfect,* she thought. She hadn't so much fun since she was a child. Free spoiled her and provided for her, but he expected her to be his girl. She was Free's Bonnie, but Britain treated her like his Coretta. He placed her on a pedestal and treated her like a lady. He left the street persona in the streets and with her he was just himself. *Next lifetime,* she thought.

She lay on her back, her hair in her face, and he was on his knees beside her as they passed the bottle back and forth.

"I missed this, ma—this is what my life has been missing. First and foremost, you're my friend," Britain stated.

Six smiled at his words because she knew exactly what he meant. "I haven't had a good friend in a long time either. I know I didn't remember you at first, but I honestly don't know how I could have ever forgotten. You're special to me, Britain," she said as she touched his face. "If I have ever done or ever do anything to hurt you, know that it's not in my heart."

Britain shook his head and took the Patrón from her hand. "You're drunk, ma . . . getting all sensitive on me," he said with a smile.

She smiled back. "Whatever, boy—I can drink you under the table. . . . You don't know whose daughter I am?"

Britain looked at the remaining liquor in the bottle. It was almost gone . . . and Six had consumed a good amount of it. "I know whose daughter you are, killa," he teased. He stood to his feet. "I'm going to grab you something eat out of the kitchen. You drank a lot. . . .You need something in your stomach."

Six threw up a peace sign and rested her eyes, closing them momentarily until Britain came back with her food.

Britain whipped her up a light sandwich and grabbed a bottled water, but when he walked back into the great room, she was already asleep.

"Six," he called out.

"Uh-huh," she answered without opening her eyes.

"You need to eat a little bit for me a'ight?" he responded.

"Hmm, hmm," she said. She sat up slightly and took a deep breath, feeling the effects of the liquor. "I'ma be so tore up in the morning."

Britain shook his head. "Nah, ma, you'll be cool. Just eat something for me," he stated as he fed her the sandwich. She ate half of it, and he made her drink the entire bottle of water. "Take these," he said as he handed her two Tylenols. She opened her mouth, and he gave them to her, then she was out like a light.

Britain retrieved linens from the guest bedroom and made sure Six, was comfortable, tucking her in as if she were a child. As he watched her chest rise and fall he was sure that he wanted her for himself. She was holding back, but on the occasions when she slipped and went all in, he felt her reciprocating his interests. He didn't know why she wouldn't take the leap and be with him, but he would wait as long as she needed him to. *She's worth it,* he thought as he leaned over her. He kissed her forehead and then retreated to his room to retire for the night.

# Chapter Twelve

Free scooped the eggs with a fork and slid it into his mouth as Lou sat across from him. The small diner was nearly empty, and cigarette smoke filled the air.

"How is Six coming with ol' boy?" Lou asked as he dug into his pancakes.

"I don't know. She's supposed to have called me last night, and she never did," Free responded as he began to think about all the reasons why Six may have not called him. *She better not be fucking the nigga*, he thought as he frowned, thinking about what she was doing at that moment. He stayed by his phone all night anticipating her voice, but it never happened. Free double-checked his phone to see if she had tried to reach him, but he had no missed calls.

"She probably just got tied up. Matter fact, he probably smashed that last night," Lou said, poking fun at his best friend.

"Shut the fuck up, nigga," Free said jokingly as he lightened up. "But look, I need a plan B to get the money for these Russians. If the nigga Britain doesn't bite on the bait, we right back to square one."

"I know. That damn Russian, Claude, is an asshole too. I know he ain't going to play if we don't get the money to him in time," Lou said with a mouthful of food.

"Lou, this is my debt. I don't want you to get too caught up in it. I lost the bricks, so I should be the one worrying about it," Free said honestly, not wanting Big Lou to suffer the consequences for something he did not do.

Lou stopped eating his food and put his fork down. Free looked at Lou like he was insane, because he never saw Lou's big ass take a break when eating. "Man, you know me better than that. You my nigga for life. Your beef is my beef. We in this together, and nobody can tell me different. Before you got knocked, you hit me with all the bricks and shared the wealth with ya boy. I was rolling with you then, so I'm going to roll with you now. Straight up!" Lou said as he picked up his fork and began to eat again.

"No doubt, fam," Free said as he nodded in agreement with his friend. Lou was a real nigga, and Free respected him and vice versa. Just as

Free began to eat his eggs, he noticed someone come through the door.

"There she go," Free whispered as he stared at the woman entering. Lou looked back and noticed Sparkle come in with big shades and tight jeans on, which hugged her curves. She began to look around the diner, searching for them. Free raised his hand and waved it to let her know where they were sitting.

"What's she doing here?" Lou whispered as he turned back around and looked at Free.

"She's my plan B," Free said as he winked at Lou and scooted over in his seat to make room as Sparkle approached.

"Hey Free," Sparkled said as she walked up and popped her gum loudly. She swung her wide hips and sat next to Free. "Hey, Lou," she said as she did a quick wave. Free smiled as he looked at Sparkle's enticing body and knew that she was perfect for the job.

"What up, ma?" Free said. Lou nodded, greeting her as he remained silent and continued to eat.

"So, what's up?" Sparkle asked as she took off her glasses and displayed her green eyes, obviously contacts.

"Like I was saying on the phone this morning . . . I got a way to make some paper. I know some niggas that's getting that paper in Pontiac, and I want you to help me hit them," Free said as he rubbed his hands together.

"Do Six know about this?" Sparkle asked skeptically as she squinted her eyes.

"No, and she doesn't need to know about this either. This is between me and you, Sparkle. She is busy doing some other shit for me right now," Free stated.

"So, what do I have to do?" Sparkle asked as she became interested. She had always had a secret crush on Free, and she was happy just to be around him without Six being in their presence. She looked him in the eyes and blushed as she thought about how fine he was.

*Damn, that was easy,* Free thought as he noticed how quickly Sparkle grew interested. He also noticed the way she was looking at him, and he sort of figured that Sparkle had a thing for him. "Well, you have to do whatever it takes. Fuck, suck, or whatever it takes to get the nigga where I need him to be," Free said bluntly, not beating around the bush whatsoever.

"What's the split?" Sparkle asked, already knowing the deal. She was not green to the game, and she wanted to lay everything out before she agreed to participate.

"Fifty-fifty," Free lied. He would never let Sparkle know how much he would really rob from the hustler he had in mind. He would just give her what he wanted to give her at the end of the caper.

"Cool," Sparkle said as she licked her lips and put her glasses back on. "What else I got to do?" she whispered as she looked at Free and ran her tongue over her top lip seductively and slowly as she slipped her hand on his thigh and gave him a light squeeze. Free moved her hand and responded.

"That's all," he said as he didn't even give her the respect to make eye contact with her. "Big Lou! Let's roll," Free instructed as he went into his pocket and dropped a twenty on the table. Sparkle scooted out, and Free followed. Lou stuffed the last bit of food into his mouth and also got up. As they headed to the door, Free stopped in his tracks and turned around. He went back to the table and scooped the twenty off it, remembering that he owed Claude so much money. *Every dollar counts*, he thought as he stuffed the money in his pocket and exited. His mind was on his next hit, a nigga named Harold from Pontiac.

\*\*\*

Lou and Free watched as Harold popped bottles and partied with his crew. The Pontiac Club was packed, and Harold had two girls hanging off of him as he partied and flossed like there was no tomorrow. Free had his hat pulled down low, almost covering his eyes. Big Lou didn't hide his face, since Harold had never met him before. Free, on the other hand, used to supply Harold with bricks of cocaine before he got locked up. Now that Free was on a paper chase, anybody was game. Free was going after every major player that he used to supply. He went from the top of the totem pole in the drug game as a supplier, to now being at the bottom as a stickup kid. The game was funny like that, but Free had no choice. He sipped on cranberry juice as if it was liquor, and Lou did the same, wanting to stay on point and focused without looking out of place.

"That's his man, Pooh Bear, that's next to him chilling," Free said as he brought the cup to his mouth and discreetly pointed with his pinkie as he took a sip. "If he is anything like he used to be, he stays strapped," Free said referring to the brown-skinned, slim guy with a small gap in his front teeth who was seated next to their mark.

Free remembered how Harold used to run through the bricks, so he was the first target once Free decided to go the ski-masked way. He also remembered how big of a trick Harold was. Harold always had a different chick on his arm and a full supply of Ecstasy pills when Free met with him in the past. Harold was considered a sex addict by everyone who knew him. Free knew this would be an easy hit because Harold always thought with his little head, rather than the one that sat on his shoulders.

Sparkle walked into the club with stilettos on and a mean walk. She wore tight-fitting, skinny jeans that showed off her wide hips and low hanging, plump cheeks. She wore her hair down and her Chinese bangs were cut perfectly across her forehead. All eyes were on her as she strutted across the floor and took a seat at the bar a couple of stools down from Harold and his entourage. Just as Free expected, Harold quickly focused his attention on Sparkle's voluptuous ass.

"Got 'em," Free whispered to Lou as he looked on and watched Sparkle work her magic. Harold whispered something to one of his goons, and he quickly approached Sparkle on his behalf.

"Let me get a shot of Patrón," Sparkle yelled as she leaned over the counter, making her cleavage push together and on full display for everyone to see. As the bartender poured a shot of the tequila in a glass for her, Sparkle casually glanced over the room and saw Free and Lou sitting in the corner of the club. She pretended as if she didn't see them and focused back on the bartender pouring her drink. Sparkle saw a man approaching her from her peripheral view and focused her attention on him. The goon wore an all-black hoodie and a NY-fitted cap turned backward with a slight lean to the right.

"Hey, how you doing, ma?" he asked as he leaned his back on the bar and propped his elbows on the countertop. He went into his pocket and dropped a hundred-dollar bill down for the bartender.

"Thanks," Sparkle said as she took the shot like a pro and ordered the bartender to give her another one.

"Oh, I see you a gangster, huh?" the man asked, impressed by her braveness in taking the shots.

"I'm a big girl," Sparkle confirmed as she displayed her perfect white smile.

"But check this out. My man Harold wants you to go up to the VIP with us. We about to head up in a minute," the man said as he slid a toothpick in his mouth and maneuvered it around with his tongue.

"Who is Harold?" Sparkle asked as she glanced over at the crowd of men. She was pretending, because she already knew exactly who he was. The three of them had been watching him for the past forty-eight hours, and she was just playing possum.

"He's the man over there with the ice on. He's the man around here," the goon said confidently as he threw his head in the direction of the crowd.

"I see him. He's cute. Why couldn't he come over here?" Sparkle asked while smiling.

"We don't move like that. He wants you to go up to VIP and meet him up there. He likes you," he said. "You game?" he asked.

"Sure," Sparkle said as she stood up and took the second shot of Patrón. Then she followed the goon up to the VIP.

When Sparkle arrived upstairs, unopened bottles of expensive champagne decorated the spacious room and a red sectional couch was in the middle of the floor. She made her way over to the couch and got comfortable. The goon sat next to her and moments later in came a crowd, with Harold in the middle of the group.

"I have to use the bathroom. Where is it?" she asked the goon as she set her purse in her lap. He threw his head toward the back of the room where the bathroom was located, and she quickly got up before the people crowded the room.

Sparkle hurried into the bathroom and pulled out her phone to call Free. She remained cool and collected as she placed the phone to her ear after opening each stall to make sure she was alone in the bathroom.

"Okay, I'm going to get that nigga to the room. This is going to be easy," Sparkle said as she smiled and fixed her hair with her free hand.

"Cool. Lou and I are going to head to the room right now and wait for y'all. Stick to the plan," Free said, reminding Sparkle to stay focused.

"I got you. I ain't new to this, I'm true to this," she said arrogantly as she looked in the mirror at herself.

"Yeah, yeah. Whatever. We waiting!" Free said, unimpressed, remembering the first time she had led him to a nigga with a pocketful of ones.

"Free, after this is done, you got something for me?" Sparkle asked invitingly as the Patrón was kicking in. She wanted to suck on Free so bad, and she wanted to feel his warmth inside of her. The stories Six had told her about his sex game had her curious and craving his stroke. Free hung up the phone, not feeding into Sparkle's nonsense. The only thing on his mind was the money and Six. Sexing Sparkle was the furthest thing on his brain at that point.

Sparkle entered the room and saw that Harold was waiting on the couch for her.

"Hey, beautiful girl," Harold said in a drunken slur and a bottle of champagne in his hands.

"Hey," Sparkle said as she sat down next to him and laid her hand on his chest.

Harold was drunk out of his mind and the sight of Sparkle's body had him thinking about giving her back shots later that night. He groped her drunkenly, and Sparkle put on a fake smile as if she was enjoying his wandering hands.

"I'm going to cut to the chase. I'll buy that pussy," Harold whispered to her as he grabbed a handful of breast.

"This ain't going to be cheap," Sparkle said, whispering in his ear.

"Money ain't shit to me," Harold said as he reached into his pocket and pulled out a wad of cash, thumbing through the bills, revealing all big faces. Sparkle's eyes grew as she looked at his wealth.

"That paper making my pussy wet," she said. Harold couldn't control himself. He felt his manhood rising. He stood up and with one hand grabbed Sparkle's hand and with the other hand, he grabbed his throbbing shaft. He pulled her up and toward the bathroom. Once they got into the bathroom, Harold's dick was already out and veins stuck out of it. Sparkle was taken by surprise and she saw the passionate look in his eyes.

"Hold on. You gotta come off that cash first," she said as she held her hand out, trying to buy her more time to think.

She had to figure out a sly way to get him to the room without his goons.

"I told you I got you," Harold said as he stroked himself. He reached into his pocket and pulled out a pill. Sparkle knew that it was Ecstasy by the way it looked. Harold took it without even taking any water with it as he continued to stroke himself, becoming rock hard and pulsating.

"Here," Harold said as he placed the pill in Sparkle's mouth. She took the pill and placed it under her tongue, pretending that she swallowed it. Then she dropped to her knees and swiftly spit it in her hand while she positioned herself to give him head. She took him into her mouth, and Harold threw his head back in pleasure as he palmed the back of her head.

Sparkle gripped Harold's pole with one hand and cuffed his balls with the other one. She massaged his balls as she sucked him off, twisting her grip on his pole as if she was revving up a Harley-Davidson. Harold was in heaven as he pumped back, feeling more freaky now that the Ecstasy was kicking in, along with the large amount of liquor he had been drinking.

"Ooh, baby. You the best," he said as he looked down at her full lips being stretched from being around his pole. All of a sudden, Sparkle stopped and began to rub her titties as she pulled one out, exposing her big, dark brown nipple.

"I'm horny as hell," she crooned. Harold loved her freaky nature, and he didn't even know her name. He was ready to dive into her and try out that fat ass.

"Pull yo' pussy out," he requested as he reached down and pinched her erect nipple.

"I can't do it in here. I have to be comfortable so I can feel this big dick. I got a room around the corner for the night. Let's just slip out and go there," she suggested as she began kissing his manhood while she continued to rub his testicles.

"Come on, ma," Harold said in a pleading tone. "Let's do it right here. I'll pay double," he bargained as he steady pumped, hitting Sparkle on the cheek and nose.

"Fuck the money. I want some of this big dick. This one is on the house, fa real," she said, knowing that stroking a man's ego was much more effective than stroking his dick. Harold smiled as he felt like the king of the world.

"Come on. Let's slip out the back," Harold said, only thinking about sex.

*This is easier than I thought*, Sparkle thought as she took one more lick on his lollipop and stood up. She put her breast back in her shirt and slowly opened the door, leading the way to the back entrance. They slipped out without anyone seeing them do so. Harold was so high, he didn't think straight. He would always put Pooh Bear on notice if he was going somewhere just to be safe. But he was blinded by lust and Sparkle's ass had a way of knocking cautious men off their square.

### Twenty-two Minutes Later

"Where the spot at?" Free yelled as the blood from Harold's kneecaps leaked onto the hotel's floor. Free had put two bullets in Harold already, and he still refused to tell him where his stash spot was at. Sparkle was putting on her clothes, and Lou sat there and watched as Free interrogated their mark.

"Okay, I see you want to play tough, huh?" Free said as he circled around Harold who was bound to a chair by rope with his hands tied behind his back. Free unzipped Harold's pants and exposed his limp dick. He yanked it with all his might and then placed the gun right under his balls. "Okay, I'm going to ask you one more time. If you don't come up off that information, I'm going to make you a woman."

"All right! All right!" Harold said in between whimpers. "It's at my spot off of I-75. I keep all my cash in a safe that I had built behind a painting," he admitted as he dropped his head and cried like a baby.

Free and Lou looked at each other and smiled. They knew that they had broken him down.

"Untie this mu'fucka! He about to take us to the spot," Free said as he let go of Harold's dick and walked to the bathroom to wash his hands.

"Time to get money," Big Lou said as Free faded into the bathroom.

Free, Lou, and Sparkle walked into Free's apartment with big smiles on their faces. They had just got back from Harold's and they were $43,000 dollars richer. Free was lightweight disappointed, though he thought for sure that Harold would have had more than forty stacks, but he took it for what it was. He left Harold's body slumped after he took them to the money. He believed that murder was a small price to pay to get him closer to his goal of paying off Claude.

"Yo, I'm about to go home. I'm tired as hell. I will be here first thing in the morning," Lou said as he felt fatigue kicking in.

"All right, my nigga," Free said as he locked hands with his best friend and embraced him.

"'Bye, Big Lou," Sparkle said as she put her hand over her mouth, yawning.

"One!" Lou said as he walked out of the door and put up two fingers. Free closed and locked the door behind him. He couldn't wait to count the money. He walked over to the table and dumped it out. Sparkled followed him. He regretted letting Sparkle come in with him. Now he couldn't lie about how much he had gotten from Harold. He owed a third of the take. *Fuck*, he thought as Sparkle began to count the money right along with him.

Free grabbed a stack of bills and putting the money in thousand-dollar stacks.

"Put them in G stacks," Free coached her, referring to thousand-dollar stacks.

"Nigga, I know how to do this," Sparkle said as she sifted through the money, not breaking her concentration or count. She glanced over at Free once she was done with the current stack, and her pussy grew moist. She got up and Free was so busy counting the money, he didn't even notice her stand behind him. Sparkle quickly took off her clothes and lay out on the table over all the money, her pussy directly in Free's face.

"What the—" Free said as he scooted back in his chair once he noticed her nakedness. Free felt his manhood rise in his jeans, but quickly dismissed the notion when he thought about her being Six's friend. "Fuck you doing?" he asked harshly as he stood up. "Put your clothes back on!" he said as he walked over to the door and opened it. "It's time for you to go," he said. Sparkle was so embarrassed and couldn't believe that Free had turned her down. That had never happened to her before.

"What the fuck is wrong with you? You a faggot or something?" Sparkle said as she heatedly got off the table and slid back in her jeans.

"I'm far from being a faggot, ma. I'm just cool on what you trying to do. This is all business, baby," Free said while never even looking at Sparkle's body. She stormed past him with a major attitude, switching her ass as hard as she could.

"Meet me here in the morning around ten. We got another hit on this nigga from Flint. Ten o'clock!" Free yelled as he watched Sparkle storm off and get into her car, noticing how her fat ass switched as he admired her shape. He quickly closed the door and shook his head, not believing that she put herself out there like that. In the looks department, Sparkle was a bad bitch, but she had nothing else going for her. "Hood rat," he mumbled as he smiled and got back to the money.

He began to think about Six and decided that he would head over to Jones's house to pay her a visit. He hadn't spoken to her, which he found odd. Even while he had been in prison they spoke almost every day. For her to go so long without contacting him worried Free, and he wanted to find out what was going on. The last thing he needed was to lose touch with her while she was in Britain's presence.

He grabbed his keys, secured the money underneath his bed, and headed out the door. He was going to check on his girl and make sure she was still down with the plan.

# Chapter Thirteen

Six crept into her father's house at six o'clock in the morning. She didn't want to wake him and also did not want him asking questions about where she had been. She had been MIA for the past two weeks, investing a lot of time into Britain. She had been having so much fun with him that she had not even thought of checking in with her father or bothering to call Free. Getting to know Britain had been a pleasure. He was showing her the side of him that the streets rarely saw, and she enjoyed his company. He introduced her to a way of life that even Free had not afforded her.

Britain was on an entirely different level than the average hustler. His money was long, and his heart was open to Six, so he shared whatever he had with her, sparing no expense to keep her happy. He had removed the gangster visage and had become her friend again. He was her courtier, her confidant, and was trying to earn the spot as her lover.

Everything with Britain felt so brand-new. He worshipped the ground beneath her feet, making her feel special without sweating her too much. He knew how to show just the right amount of affection. He let her know how much she meant to him without smothering her or appearing needy, and slowly, he had warmed his way into her cold heart. What started out as business was slowly becoming personal, even though she was aware that their relationship could never go too far.

There was no future for them. They had to live in the present because their days were numbered, and after she executed Free's plan, Britain would never look at her the same way ever again.

Her attraction to Britain was so different than anything she had ever felt for Free. With Free she was his girl. His ride or die . . . Bonnie to his Clyde. Their relationship was one that the hood recognized. She was his wifey. With Britain, however, she was his lady. He didn't want a girl—he wanted a woman and was stepping to her with such sophistication that it blew Six's mind. He had her open.

It was so dark inside the house that Six bumped into the coffee table, knocking all of the contents off of it and breaking through the silence in the still house.

All of a sudden, her father's voice cut through the air. "I don't know what you creeping for," he stated. "I'm not the one who has been waiting on you to come home."

Six's eyes adjusted to the darkness, and she saw her father sitting in his chair.

"I wasn't creeping, Daddy . . . I'm grown. I just didn't want to wake you up," she lied, feeling as if she were a teenager again.

"Hmm, hmm, I hear you . . . but like I said, I'm not the one who you need to be worried about," he answered as he stood to his feet. He walked over to Six and kissed her on the cheek as he passed by. "I'm going to bed, but Free is waiting for you in your bedroom. He's been here all night."

Six's heart rate increased at the thought of Free. She knew him well and already knew that he was furious because he had not heard from her. She turned her head and stared nervously at her closed bedroom door. She was more afraid to face him then she had been her father. Intimidation filled her, and she tried to think of an excuse to tell Free.

"Go on in there. You were grown just a second ago," Jones teased. "You got to deal with it sooner or later. You've been running around here with Britain like you're really his girl. You've got to keep your head in the game, baby girl. Remember who you belong to. It's all about the money," Jones reminded her as he disappeared into his own room.

Six took a deep breath and entered her room. She flicked on the light to find Free sitting in a chair, glaring at her. It looked like he had been up all night, and the worry on his face instantly transformed to wrath as soon as he saw that she was all right. His temple pulsated as he ground his teeth in anger.

"Where you been, Six?" His question was simple, but Six remained silent, because she really did not know what to tell him. He knew where she had been and what she had been doing. *What does he want me to say?* she thought as she moved closer to him.

"I've been with Britain," she replied as she stood in front of him.

He stood and held the bridge of his nose, attempting to keep his composure. "You ain't been back here for weeks. You haven't returned any of my calls. . . . Why you ain't been checking in with me?" he grilled.

Free was so upset that Six could see the fire in his eyes. She sighed because she knew that she was wrong, but she couldn't play wifey to two men at the same time. A man knew when his woman's heart was torn. If Free wanted the job done right, he was going to have to give her space.

"I've been kind of busy, Free. I can't be answering my phone for you every time you call. I'm supposed to be acting like his girl. I have to concentrate on him right now so that I can get him to trust me. It's just an act," she said unconvincingly.

Free looked her over, taking in her new appearance. Everything about her had changed. She was more refined, more graceful . . . less hood then he remembered. The girl standing before him was not the little ghetto girl he had fallen in love with. Even her hair color was different. He looked at the designer labels she wore, and as his eyes scanned her body, he saw the twinkle of diamonds around her neck. Six was rocking the ten-karat diamond necklace that Britain had given her. It was the perfect accessory to the new queen of the streets. She shined like royalty, and Free became enraged.

"Bitch, what the fuck is this around your neck?" he asked as he stepped to Six, pinning her against the bedroom door while sticking a threatening finger in her face. Hitting her never crossed his mind. He had never raised a hand to her, but he felt like she was disrespecting him by flaunting the jewels in his face that Britain had given her.

"Nigga, get your finger out of my face!" Six yelled as she slapped his hand away. "What the fuck is wrong with you?" she asked, still pinned between Free and the door.

"This nigga icing you out now? You Britain's bitch now?" he asked. "That's twenty grand around your neck, Six. A man don't spend that type of money on a bitch unless he fucking her."

"Fuck you, Free! You're the one who asked me to do this in the first place . . . of course, he buys me things. You wanted me to be wifey, remember? Well, I am! He treats me like wifey . . . he buys me shit, expensive shit! You put me in this situation, Free, so don't act like you can't handle it now. Isn't this what you wanted? You started this entire fucked-up game," she defended with anger.

"I told you not to fuck him!" Free screamed. "I didn't know you were going to get blinded by the money, but I forgot . . . a ho is gon' be a ho when it's all said and done."

*Smack!*

Out of nowhere, Six slapped Free with all of her might as tears formed in her eyes. Out of all the years she had been with him, he had never called her out of her name. It was the one thing that they always had for each other: respect. Him referring to her in such a derogatory way crushed her heart. She shook her head and squinted as she stared at him as if she didn't even know who was standing in front of her.

"Fuck you, Free," Six whispered as she pushed him off of her and walked over to her bed. She sat down and put her face in her hands as she let the tears roll down her face.

Free punched the wall and shook his head as he tried to tone down his temper. "I can't believe you fucked this nigga, ma." His stomach turned at just the thought of another man inside of her. He was sick thinking about it. She was supposed to be his, and the sting of betrayal threatened to break him down at any moment.

Free had tested his limits with Six on numerous occasions by being unfaithful, but he called himself just being a nigga. His heart never waned away from Six. Emotionally and mentally, he belonged to her. In his mind, women could not separate sex from love. To have his woman intimate with another man was the ultimate slap in the face.

"I didn't fuck him," Six replied sadly. "I would never do that to you. The only reason I'm even doing this is for us . . . because you convinced me to."

She could see it in his eyes that he didn't believe her and that was what hurt her the most.

"Fuck that—you're done. You're out. I'll get the money another way," Free insisted. The tone of his voice still reflected his fury, and he looked at her as if she were diseased.

"What way, Free? If you don't come up with the dough, you're dead and so am I. I'm not chancing my life like that. Hitting Britain is the only way to do this, and you know it. You need to put your ego aside and let me finish this." Six was trying her hardest to convince Free to see things her way, but inside, she secretly wondered if her head was in the right place. She could not see herself giving Britain up right now. Life with him was so easy, so carefree. He was a good man, and she felt guilty that he had even gotten caught up in a beef with Free. He was a target and did not even know it.

By the time Britain realized he had gotten robbed, Free and Six planned to be in the wind. They would be like a distant memory to Detroit. A part of her wished that Britain would not have fallen for her—that way she would not be the one to have to betray him, but his affection for her was his weakness. When it was time for her to let him go, she would, but until then, she was going to enjoy the ride while it lasted.

"Sounds to me like you're too attached to this mu'fucka," Free stated harshly.

"It's not about that, Free!" Six objected.

"Then what is all of this—" he pointed to her outfit, waving his finger up and down. "What is this about?"

"He likes me this way. I have to be who he likes," Six said in a low voice.

"What about the Six I like?" he asked as he looked at her in disappointment.

"Right now, she doesn't exist. I'm changing what I have to change to get the job done. I'm doing what you asked of me," she replied.

Free shook his head. "You need to remind yourself whose team you're on," he spat and began to leave. Six tried to grab his hand to stop him, but he snatched away from her and slammed the door on his way out.

"Free!" she called after him as she ran out of the room to follow behind him, but by the time she hit the front porch, he was already pulling away from the house. His tires squealed as he pulled off down the street.

"Let him cool down," Jones said from behind her. "He loves you, so he doesn't know no other way to feel but jealous."

"He has nothing to be jealous of, Daddy. I'm in and out of there as soon as I get the cash. I'm not feeling Britain. I have always loved Free. He should know that," Six stated adamantly as she pulled her hair back into a ponytail while lines of worry creased her forehead.

"You sure about that?" Jones questioned as he took a seat on the couch. "The way you've been carrying on, I would have thought differently. Britain is a nice kid. I love him like a son, but you chose Free. I always told you to be sure before you pledged your allegiance to a nigga, because once a man give you his heart, you're his. It takes a lot for a man to let go of what he thinks he's entitled to."

"I'm not asking Free to let go," Six replied. She flopped down next to her father and rested her head on his shoulder.

"But you're allowing Britain to hold on too. You're being pulled in two different directions, baby girl."

"It's all an act, Daddy. Free just has to give me space. Britain is smart. If he even suspects that I still deal with Free, this entire thing will be over. Then what? We need this money. Free has to remember the plan and stick to it. After it's all said and done, Britain is the one who ends up with the broken heart. Free has nothing to worry about."

Jones patted the top of his daughter's head. "If you ever feel like you can't handle it, you call me. I know you're in between a rock and a hard place right now, but your daddy will rock both of them li'l niggas to sleep if either of them step too far out of line. You be careful. Britain is more like his father than you realize. If he finds out about what you're doing, things can get real ugly."

"He won't find out, Daddy; at least, not until I'm long gone. He wouldn't hurt me anyway . . . you don't know him like I do. I am the one who is going to hurt him; that's what so fucked-up about it," Six replied with a heavy heart.

# Chapter Fourteen

Six stood in the mirror and applied mascara onto her lashes as she dolled herself up. She canceled her date with Britain so that she could surprise Free with a sexy little show. *I have been neglecting Free, and I just want him to remember where home is,* she thought as she stepped back and looked at herself in the full-length mirror. She hadn't been spending time with Free lately, and it seemed as if she was forgetting what the main objective was . . . and that was to rob Britain blind.

Six looked at her oiled up legs and smiled as she admired her six-inch stilettos she wore along with a red see-through lingerie piece. She smiled as she made sure her long curls were in place, which was Free's favorite hairstyle of hers. Then she picked up the trench coat that she had on the bed and grabbed her night bag as she headed out of her father's house.

"I will see you later, Daddy. Don't wait up for me," Six yelled as she headed out the door and made her way over to the apartment to surprise Free with a much-needed sexual escapade.

Free was in the motel's bathroom, washing blood off his hands and face. He had just left Flint and managed to hit a former friend, Jimmy, for two bricks of cocaine and just over twenty thousand cash. Sparkle had once again set up a former customer of his, and the end result was a hustler being dead and Free being richer. That particular time, Lou wasn't with them. He was in Saginaw scoping out another potential victim for them to set up next. Sparkle was in the room waiting for Free as he cleaned himself up before heading back home to Detroit.

Free walked out with his shirt off and a drying towel, wiping his hands. His body was tattooed up and his six-pack was on point, resembling a washboard. His jail sentence allowed him to work on his body, and it had paid off tremendously. He had a body of a model but the swagger of a street hustler; a perfect combination in Sparkle's eyes.

"You about ready?" he asked as Sparkle counted the money on the bed.

"Yeah, I'm ready. There's about twenty-one thousand dollars in here," she said as she loaded the money back into the duffel bag, smiling.

"I tell you what. You keep the money. I will take the coke," Free said, hoping that Sparkle would fall for it. He knew that the bricks were worth twenty-five thousand apiece on the street, and he would be getting the good end of the stick if he took the drugs rather than the money.

"How much are the bricks worth?" Sparkle asked as she sat Indian-style on the bed.

"'Bout ten thousand apiece," Free lied.

Sparkle began to chuckle and shook her head from side to side as she leaned back on her hands.

"What's so funny?" Free asked curiously as he continued to clean himself.

"I was born on a night, but it wasn't last night. I'm not dumb, playboy. Them mu'fuckas go for about twenty-five or twenty-six in the streets right now. Who you think you playing? I have been around the corner a couple times or two," Sparkle said cockily as she opened her legs and propped them up on the bed, exposing her neatly shaved vagina that was under her skirt. She had always hated to wear panties. It was a bad habit of hers.

Free was impressed by her knowledge of the going rate for a brick of cocaine. "So, how you want to split it up?" Free asked, trying not to look at her exposed vagina. He knew that he had to come clean and be honest with her about the coke price.

"You can keep the bricks, but I want that dick," she said as she laid back and began to play with her clitoris right in front of him. She wanted Free so bad, and she was going to pursue his sex relentlessly until she got it.

Free finally looked at her large pink clitoris as she rubbed it, and he couldn't help but to get aroused. He slowly walked over to her and stood over her as she closed her eyes and masturbated right in front of him as if he wasn't even there. Her moaning and sex sounds had him hard as a missile and temptation got the best of him as he found his middle finger helping her masturbate. She was soaking wet, and Free had never experienced a woman get so drenched in his entire life. He slipped his two fingers into her and felt her warmness. His wet fingers went in and out of her, and he let his thumb begin to rub her clitoris simultaneously. He quickly pulled back when he thought about where he was at.

"We can't do this here," he whispered in a raspy tone as he realized that he was in a motel only five miles away from Jimmy's murder scene. He had just killed Jimmy in his own house and wanted to get out of Flint ASAP. "We will finish this at my house," Free said as he grabbed his hoodie and put it on.

"No, I want you now. I'm so horny," Sparkle contested as she sat up while still playing with herself, rapidly moving her two middle fingers over her clitoris.

"Sparkle! Let's go!" Free yelled as he picked up the duffel bag and grabbed his key off the dresser. Sparkle smiled, loving his authoritative tone and dominance. She promised herself that she would put it on him once they reached his home.

Free realized that if he wanted to keep getting money with Sparkle, he would have to keep her happy for the time being. He would eventually have to give her some dick, although he didn't want to start that type of relationship with her. He hated chicks like Sparkle, and on top of that, she was cool with his girl. Nevertheless, he was on his hustle by any means necessary, and he had to pay back his debt to the Russians or meet his death. He decided to go 'head and lay it on her when they got back to Detroit. *All business . . . no pleasure,* he thought to himself, trying to justify cheating on the woman he loved, Six.

*He won't even remember Six's name when I'm done with him,* Sparkle thought to herself as she pulled down her skirt, got up, and followed him out.


*Yes! He's not here,* Six thought excitedly as she walked into their apartment. She knew that he wouldn't expect her there because she had told him that she was going out with Britain on that night. *Tonight is going to be perfect,* she thought as she put her bag down and began to take out the candles and rose petals she had brought for their special night. When she took a look around the house, she noticed that the apartment was a mess.

"That boy can't clean worth shit," she said under her breath as she smiled, thinking about how she would always have to clean up after him. At that particular moment, she realized how much she missed the little things that he did that made her love him so much. She missed being around him and was ready to get the robbery with Britain over with. She began to clean the house so she could prepare for his arrival. Just as she was picking up some of his sweatpants, she heard her phone ring from inside of her bag.

"Hey, baby," Free said into the phone as he heard the sound of Six on the other end.

"Hey. I miss you," Six said as she wiped off the countertops and cleaned while talking.

"I miss you too baby," Free said as he drove down the interstate toward Detroit. " Whoa!" Free yelled as he cringed and jerked back.

"What's wrong?" Six asked, concerned.

"Oh, nothing. I almost hit a damn deer," he lied. He actually was cringing because Sparkle had rubbed her teeth against his manhood while she was giving him head. He looked down at her sucking him and tried to regain his composure as she went to work on him—slurping and taking him all into her mouth while she massaged his balls.

"Oh, okay. Be careful," Six said.

"You know I will. What are you doing?" Free asked, trying to make sure she was with Britain because he was only minutes away from their apartment.

"Oh, nothing. In the bathroom at his restaurant," she lied, trying to not tip him off about her being at the apartment.

"Everything going smooth?" Free asked as he temporarily closed his eyes as he got pleased by Sparkle.

"Yeah, you know I'm going to wrap this shit up ASAP and we going to get that money," Six responded, giving him her thick New York accent.

"Cool, cool. You know I love you, girl. You are my world," Free said as he felt himself about to climax.

"I love you too," Six said as she smiled and walked into the bedroom to begin setting the mood. "Where are you?" she asked.

"I'm about to go home. I'm tired as hell. Lou and I have been in the streets all day trying to come up, feel me?" he lied.

"Okay, well, I love you, and I will call you in morning," she said sweetly.

"Get off the phone, baby," Sparkle whispered as she momentarily stopped sucking him and stroked him slowly while rubbing his tip across her full lips, all while looking up at him, displaying her big puppy dog-eyes. Free put his pointing finger over his lips, signaling her to keep quiet.

"Okay, Six. Good night," he said as he quickly flipped down his phone and let Sparkle get back to work.


Six placed each candle strategically around the bedroom and left a trail of rose petals from the front door to the room. She sipped on champagne as she tried to get prepared for Free to enter. She decided not to play any music, not wanting to tip him off as soon as he entered. The keys jingling in the door announced his presence and she quickly downed her champagne as she darted into their bedroom closet. She was going to give him the surprise of his life. Six closed the closet door and had a clear view of the bed through the shingles on the door.

Free and Sparkle passionately kissed as Free tried his best to put his key in his door. Sparkle grabbed his rock-hard pipe through his jeans and couldn't wait to feel him inside her. She was soaking wet and had an itch that desperately needed to be scratched by Free.

He finally got the door open and they stepped in together, all over each other. They continued to kiss aggressively, and Sparkle took off her clothes as they stumbled through the house, not even noticing the rose petals on the floor. Free palmed Sparkle's curvy cheeks while still French-kissing her. Her juices began to run down her leg as she felt her clitoris begin to thump in pleasure, anticipating friction.

Sparkle began to unbuckle Free's pants as he walked backward into his own bedroom. His pants dropped to the floor, exposing his soldier who stood at full attention. Sparkle pushed Free onto the bed and prowled over him like the seductress she was, preparing to take him on the ride of his life.

"Hold up, ma—a condom," Free said as he reached over onto the nightstand to retrieve one. Sparkle took it from his hand and applied the glove to his thickness, then instantly jumped on his pole. He slid into her with ease as she began riding him like she was in a rodeo. The sounds of her butt cheeks smacking against his balls echoed throughout the room loudly as she went into overdrive.

Just as Six was about to jump out the closet and yell "surprise," she got an unexpected surprise of her own. She stopped dead in her tracks, and her eyes grew as big as golf balls as she witnessed the unthinkable. Her heart had just been broken in two as she saw Sparkle riding her man and moaning while her breasts bounced up and down. Six froze as she watched another woman ride Free like a crazed sex fiend. Six's breaths got shallow and her heart rate tripled as she placed her hand on her chest and watched voyeur-style. The sadness quickly transformed into rage as Six's temperature began to rise.

"Oh, Free! This dick is so good," Sparkle complimented as she began to make her cheeks alternate bounces, moving one butt cheek up at a time while still on his pipe. She then began to rub her clitoris hastily as she ground harder and deeper on Free's pole.

"What the fuck!' Six yelled as she burst out of the closet. She couldn't take it anymore. Free and Sparkle looked at Six in total shock, not understanding what was going on until it was too late.

Free yelled, "Six!" as he scrambled and pushed Sparkle off him, causing her to fall hard onto the floor. Before he could do anything else, Six grabbed the champagne bottle that was on the side of the bed. She cocked it back like a baseball bat and whacked Sparkled dead in her forehead, causing her head to split and bleed on impact.

"Bitch! You got to be out of yo' damn mind!" Six yelled as she took the remaining broken glass that was in her hand and stabbed Sparkle in the chest with all her might. Six cut her hand also, but at that point, she didn't care. Hurting Sparkle was the only thing that mattered to her.

"Aggh!" Sparkle screamed as she grabbed her wounded chest and became woozy. Six was going for broke on Sparkle's ass. Six gave her forceful a kick to the nose, knocking her on her back and out cold instantly. Free stood up and scrambled to cover himself as he pulled his pants up nervously, while trying his best to explain.

"Six, it's not what you think. I—" Free tried to explain, but a flying champagne bottle caused him to duck and not finish his sentence.

"How could you do this to me, you grimy mu'-fucka?" Six asked as the tears began to stream down her face. She was so enraged that she couldn't catch her breath as hatred filled her heart. "How could you?" she screamed as she picked up the lamp and tossed that at him also, this time catching Free across the head.

"Hold up, baby," Free said as he put both of his hands in front of himself, trying to get her to calm down.

"I am not your baby! I hate you! I fucking hate you!" Six screamed at the top of her lungs as sweat and tears streamed down her face. Free ran over to her and tried to hug her, but Six gave him a swift and hard knee to his groin area, causing him to fold like a lawn chair. She then spit on him as he grimaced in pain on his knees right before her.

"Never call me again! I am through with you! I hate you!" she said as snatched her coat and put it over her scantily clad body. She stormed out, but not before giving an unconscious Sparkle another kick to the stomach for good measure.

"Wait, Six!" Free mumbled under his breath as the excruciating pain of his bells being rung shot up his body. "Wait!" he managed to yell, but it was no use—she was gone.

# Chapter Fifteen

"Six! Six, wait!" Free called after her as she ran to her car. She was so sick with grief that when she sat down in the driver's seat, she couldn't hold the contents of her stomach. She leaned out of the car and heaved violently as she threw up. Free finally caught up to her and knelt down in front of her. As he moved her hair out of her face, she continued to hurl.

"Don't touch me!" she screamed at the top of her lungs as she slapped his hands away. She was completely disgusted by him. To get involved with her best friend was unforgivable.

"Six, baby, just listen to me," he pleaded as he attempted to hug her.

"No," she replied, "No, don't fucking touch me. You bitch-ass nigga, I hate you!" Tears flowed freely down her cheeks. "After everything you put me through—everything that I'm doing for you! You fuck with Sparkle? My best friend? Are you fucking serious?" she asked rhetorically as she punched him in the chest.

"Baby, let me explain. I'm all fucked-up without you, ma—it wasn't what it looked like," Free said.

Six put both hands on the sides of her head and shook her head as she thought of what she had seen. "The bitch shouldn't even have been in the house! You're real friendly with Sparkle all of a sudden. You're grimy, Free, and to think I was about to set up a good nigga for you. What was I thinking? Britain would never do this to me," Six stated as she grabbed her door and slammed it closed. She put the car in drive and began to pull away.

"Six, I love you, ma—don't do this—don't fuck us up over this. It was a mistake," Free responded as he began to jog alongside the car in an attempt to stop her from leaving.

"You were a mistake," she responded as she sped off, leaving Free in her rearview mirror.

Tears burned her eyelids, and she was so distraught that she could barely see the road in front of her. She had trusted Free and had given up a lot to be with him. *I put my life on hold for three years while he was locked up!* she thought in disbelief. *Why would he do this to me?*

She pulled her car over on the side of the road to calm down and as if the world was synchronized with her life, it began to rain. It was as if God knew her sorrow and decided to cry with her.

Six broke down as she gripped the steering wheel. Nothing in her life had ever hurt so badly. The thought of Sparkle and Free together made her stomach turn in disgust. She knew in her heart that she could never forgive Free for what he had done. Yes, he had cheated on her before, but never with one of her girls. Free was *her* man, and she found it so disrespectful for him to even entertain the thought of hooking up with Sparkle. The fact that it was her best friend burned her up inside. *I had the bitch around me and Free all the time. I told her shit about my man. I trusted her,* Six thought, feeling stupid for being too naïve.

Free was supposed to be her best friend. They were more than just a couple; she had thought he was her destiny, which is why it felt like daggers were being stabbed through her chest. There was no telling how long Sparkle and Free had been fucking around. Six felt like a fool. *Were they sitting back, laughing at me the entire time?* she asked. Now that she knew the truth, it haunted her. It was something that her eyes should have never seen, but now that they had, she could not erase the image from her mind.

"I should go fuck that bitch up," Six whispered as the mixture of anger and sadness overwhelmed her, but she knew that Free was really the one to blame. He was the one who owed her something . . . they owed each other everything because they had committed to one another. "I can't believe he would do this," she muttered repeatedly while gripping her stomach. As much as she wanted to blame Sparkle, a ho could only steal your man if your man allowed her to . . . so no, she blamed Free, fully.

Her cell phone rang, and Six looked at the caller ID. She muffled her cries with the back of her wrist as she sent Free to voice mail. She did not even want to hear his voice. If she gave him the opportunity to speak, he might flip the situation and talk himself right back into her life. She shook her head stubbornly.

"No, he doesn't have shit to say to me," she coached herself as her phone rang again. This time, she hit ignore without thinking twice. There really was nothing that he could say. She had witnessed his disloyalty with her own eyes. "Here I am fucking up a good thing with a nigga who really cares for me, just to save his ass." She regained her composure and put her car back on the road. Her broken heart urged her to go home to her father. He was the one person who she knew would never hurt her, and she needed him now more than ever.

Jones had always helped her figure out her life when it was too difficult for her to navigate through alone; she only hoped that he had an answer to her current problem. He was a man with much wisdom. Surely he could some insight on Free's actions. All Six wanted to know was why. After everything . . . why?

She sped all the way home, dangerously whipping her car through the pouring rain. She had never been so unsettled in her life. Her emotions were all over the place. She felt unloved, she felt hurt, she felt abandoned. Two of the few people who she trusted had trespassed against her in the worst way. It was a pain too great to bear alone, which is why she was rushing to her father.

When Six finally pulled up to her father's home, she rushed out of the car, distraught. Rain drenched her, causing her hair to stick to her face. Her hands were so shaky that she could not find the key to open the front door.

"Daddy!" she cried as she knocked on the door, her voice resembling that of a lost child. She needed her father more than anyone else at the moment. Free had broken her heart to pieces, and Jones was the only one capable of putting it back together. She trusted her father and knew that he would be able to lay out the situation for her in a way that she would understand. He would help her make sense of it all.

She rang the doorbell, but no one answered. *Please be here,* she thought. She was soaked and trembling as she searched for the correct key. When she finally let herself in, it was pitch black inside.

"Daddy! I really need to talk to you!" she yelled as she went through the house, turning on the lights. Her mascara was smeared all down her cheeks, and the wet clothing stuck to her body as she knocked on his bedroom door. "Daddy, are you in here?" she asked as she opened the door and peeked her head inside. She could see his silhouette on the bed.

"Daddy, I'm so done with Free," she started as she flicked the light switch. The light didn't come on, so she walked inside to turn on the lamp beside his bed. "Daddy, wake up, I really need to talk—" As Six turned on the light switch, her sentence caught in her throat.

Blood soaked his bedsheets, and her dilemma with Free instantly went away when she saw her father lying with his eyes open and a bullet wound to the head.

"Daddy!" she screamed as she fell to the floor beside his bed. "Daddy, no! Please get up!" she cried as she kissed his face over and over again.

"Baby girl," she heard him whisper weakly in her ear. She looked at him in shock as she realized that he wasn't dead.

"I'm right here, Daddy. Just hold on for me," she said frantically as she grabbed the phone off the nightstand and dialed 911. "9-1-1, what is your emergency?" the operator answered. "Please, somebody help me! My father—he's been shot!" Six screamed as she cradled the phone in her neck and attempted to scoop her father in her arms. "Please!" she begged as she placed his head on her lap. His eyes stared into hers, and she dropped the phone as she concentrated on her father. Her eyes burned as the tears fell from her face and onto her father's cheeks. She wiped the wetness from his cheeks as she rocked him back and forth in her arms.

"I love you, Daddy," she whispered as she used her fingers to close his seemingly lifeless eyes. Her chest ached, and she tried to inhale, but each time she tried to suck in air a sharp pain erupted through her heart. She closed her eyes and shook her head from side to side as if she were in disbelief. "You're going to be okay . . . just hold on, old man," she pleaded as she took the sheets in her hand and pressed them up against her father's wound.

"Baby girl," he gasped. All Jones could do was look up at his beautiful daughter. The blood in his eyes partially obstructed his view of her, but he was grateful to have her voice in his ear when he needed her most. The amount of love he had for Six was so great that he didn't mind dying, as long as she was by his side. She didn't know it, but she was coaching him step-by-step as he made his way into the light.

"Don't talk, Daddy . . . stop talking. I'm here, Daddy. Just save your energy," Six said as she tried desperately to stop the blood from flowing out of his brain. There was so much blood on her hands that she knew her efforts were useless. Her father was going to die, and there was nothing that she could do to stop it.

"Hmm," he grunted as his grip loosened on her hand.

"I love you so much, Daddy—you're the shit, you know that," Six stated. "Can't nobody ever take your place, Daddy." She closed her eyes and rocked him back and forth. "Your baby girl is right here with you. If you die on me, I'm going to fuck you up," she threatened as she kissed his cheek.

"Where are they?" Six yelled in frustration, hoping the ambulance would quickly arrive.

Six felt her father let go of her hand and although his eyes were open, there was nothing but empty space behind his stare. "Daddy," she whispered as she shook him slightly. "Daddy, wake up—please, Daddy. You're all I've got!"

At that moment, the paramedics came through the door and witnessed Six holding her father in her arms. Her sobs revealed her tragedy as her body heaved violently from her cries while she gently rubbed his face.

"You're too late!" she screamed. "What the fuck took you so long!" Her screams were more like raspy wails, and blood covered her as she closed her father's eyes.

The paramedics approached her and tried to remove Jones from her grasp. "No! Don't take him yet! I just want to say good-bye!" she cried. She was no longer a grown woman, but a daddy's girl who had been crushed by her father's sudden death.

The paramedics looked at each other confused. No one wanted to be the one to separate Six from Jones. Seeing her mourning over his dead body would have brought tears to the toughest of men.

"We have to remove the body," a paramedic stated to a police officer who was entering the room.

The officer looked at Six and shook his head as the ringing of a cell phone erupted. He looked at Six's cell phone that was on the floor at her feet, along with the contents of her purse. Six recognized the ringtone. She knew it was Britain, and as the officer answered the call, she stated, "Tell him to come."

***

Britain walked into Jones's house and noticed policemen and paramedics crowded around the doorway to Jones's room.

"Six!" he yelled as he made his way toward the scene in a hurry. He pushed his way through, and when he saw what they all were looking at, he stopped midstep. Six was crying over Jones, blood saturated her clothing, and the officers were negotiating with her to release the body; she wouldn't let go.

Britain stepped closely to Six and looked down at Jones's body. *Damn,* he thought sadly. *Somebody finally caught Jones slipping.* Britain knew that karma would inevitably catch up to Jones as it did his father so many years ago. The life of a murderer for hire was never long, but he knew that this was something that Six would never understand. He kneeled beside her and stared up into her swollen eyes.

"Six, it's time to let him go," he whispered as the silent crowd around him watched glumly.

Six shook her head. "I can't. I'm his daughter. He needs me," she responded with her eyes still focused on Jones.

"He wouldn't want you to see him like this, ma. There's nothing you can do for him now," Britain replied softly as he put his hand on her cheek, brushing the bloody hair out of her face. "Let him go, Six. Let the men do their jobs and take care of him."

"He's my daddy," Six whispered. "Who would do this to him?" she asked as she looked up into Britain's eyes.

Britain didn't want to tell her the truth . . . he didn't want to tell her that Jones himself had done this to many other niggas and had robbed many other little girls out of their time with their fathers. He simply shook his head and replied, "You've got to let go, ma."

Six nodded her head and choked up again as she brought her father close to her chest one last time. "The last real nigga on earth just died. I love you," she whispered before allowing the paramedics to remove his body. She stood to her feet, but the world spun beneath her, and she collapsed in Britain's arms.

Britain carried Six out of the house, and she clung to him desperately as he placed her in his car. She cried silently the entire way to his home. Britain did not know what to say to quell her pain, so he didn't say anything at all. When his father died, he hated hearing the million apologies from people who could never understand.

He didn't want to be another useless voice in her ear. He wasn't going to tell her that it would be all right because he knew for a fact that the pain never went away. Six would feel the loss of her father for the rest of her life. All he could do was help her bear this new cross.

He reached over and grabbed her hand as he whipped his car through the city streets. When Six felt Britain wrap her hand in his, she squeezed it tightly, hanging on for dear life. In one night she had lost both of the men in her life. She had lost Free due to mistrust, and she had been robbed of her father by the streets. As she stared out of the window, she realized that Britain was not the man she planned to be with, but he was the one who was here, by her side, when she most needed him.

Britain pulled up to his Grosse Pointe Woods estate. He pressed the numeric keypad on his steering wheel, and the gates opened, welcoming them into his castle.

He helped her out of the car and into the house, where he removed her clothing. As he pulled her shirt over her head he wished he could take away some of her grief.

"Lift your leg, ma," he whispered as he removed her jeans.

He put her clothes in a plastic bag and tossed it in the trash.

"No," she whispered, reaching her hand out to stop him. "Don't just throw them away."

Britain nodded, understanding that she was trying to hold on to every little piece of her father. He retrieved the bag and replied, "I'll have them cleaned for you."

She stood in his great room in just her panties and bra and pulled at her hair as she closed her eyes. Britain picked her up and carried her up the stairs to his bedroom and into the master bath. He turned on the shower, then kicked off his shoes before he stepped inside with Six still in his arms.

"Stand up for me, baby girl," Britain spoke. When he called her by the same nickname that her father had given her, she broke down all over again.

The water hit her body as her father's blood swirled down the drain. She sobbed with her face in her hands. Britain allowed her to cry as he grabbed a loofah and softly washed her body. He paid attention to every part of her body to make sure that he didn't leave a trace of blood, even washing her hair. By the time he was done he was soaking wet, but the Armani slacks could be replaced. Six was important to him, and he knew that right now she needed to be catered to. She was fragile and vulnerable. He made it his personal mission to make sure this didn't destroy her.

After drying her body and lotioning her down from head to toe, he dressed her in a nightgown that she had left at his house. He tucked her in and whispered, "I'm here if you need me."

Six did not respond. She simply stared at the wall as a lone tear escaped and fell onto her pillow. She heard Britain leave the room, and she balled her fist and bit her finger to stop herself from crying too loudly. She knew that sleep would not come easy that night because all she would see in her head was her father's bloody face.

Britain closed his eyes as he removed his wet clothing and sat down on the bed. He couldn't believe that Jones had been killed. The devastation that he saw in Six is what hurt him the most. *She's never going to get over this,* he thought as he lay back in his bed and rubbed his goatee. He could hear her crying in the next room, and the pit of his stomach felt hollow just knowing that she was suffering. He was feeling Six and had grown closer to her than any other woman he had ever been with. He never wanted to see her this way, and as much as he wanted to give her space, her cries were like a magnet—they drew him near. He put his robe on over his pajama pants and went back into his guestroom.

Six heard him open the door and although her back was turned to him, she could feel his presence.

"Hold me," she requested.

Britain got into the bed with Six and wrapped his arms around her, causing her crying to cease. He rubbed her back in tiny circles for hours before she finally drifted to sleep. As Britain lay in bed with her in his arms, he thought, *This is how it's supposed to be.* With her next to him, he found peace, but he knew that it was only temporary, because before he could fully own Six's heart, he would have to mend it.

Six awoke to a full breakfast platter sitting on the side of the bed, but her appetite was nonexistent. She heard her phone ring, and she reached over to grab it off the nightstand. It was Free. As soon as she saw his name pop up on her caller ID, she sent him to voice mail. *There's nothing left to say,* she thought angrily as she went into the bathroom and looked in the mirror. Her eyes were puffy and red. Her tears had created ashy trails down her golden face. She brushed her teeth and rinsed her face with cold water before wrapping herself in Britain's robe, exiting the room.

Making her way down the marble corridor, she felt as if she would throw up. She still hadn't wrapped her mind around what had happened. She started down the glass stairs to find Britain directing some of his goons into the house. They were carrying bags from all of her favorite department stores and placing them in the living room. There had to be over fifty bags in the space: Macy's, Bloomingdale's, Saks, Tiffany's . . . all of the designer bags filled the room.

"Britain?" she said unsurely as she descended the rest of the stairs.

He turned around and looked at her with concern. "Good morning, ma," he said as he extended his hand to help her down the last step. He kissed the top of her head.

"What is going on?" she asked.

"Everything you will need is here. From new clothes to tampons," he stated. "I don't want you to ever have to go back there. I've made arrangements to have your father's place cleaned up, and I instructed them to box all of your father's belongings and have them shipped here. You can go through them when they get here to choose what you would like to keep. I've already taken care of the funeral arrangements, and you can stay here with me as long as you like."

Six leaned against him as he put his arm around her shoulders. "This is your home now. There is nothing I can't give you, Six. I just want to make you happy, ma," he said.

She nodded and whispered, "You're too good for me. Thank you for everything, Britain."

After everything was in the house, all of his workers left and Britain sat down on the plush leather sofa, pulling Six down into his arms. He cradled her like a baby as he stroked her hair.

"You want to talk about it?" he asked.

"I just can't believe he's gone," she uttered. "He was my life."

"What would you say if I asked you to build a new life with me?" Britain stated. He wanted to get everything out in the open. He was falling in love with Six, and he wanted her for himself. Jones's death reminded him that life was too short and he didn't have time to waste. The life he was leading could be a lonely one. Being king meant nothing if he did not have a queen to share his world with.

As Six's head rested against Britain's chest, she could hear his heart beating anxiously as he awaited her answer. Free popped into her mind, and she forced herself to push him out. As much as she wanted to be with Free, she couldn't trust him. What he had done was unacceptable. She had held him down from the very beginning, and although he had not always been faithful, she had never questioned his love for her. She attributed his cheating ways to a nigga just being a nigga, but after everything—after holding him down while he was in prison, after proving to him that her love was unconditional— she expected so much more from him. After all that she had given of herself, she expected his loyalty in return.

Free's actions made it so much easier for Six to love Britain. She had fought her feelings for him long enough. Now that her father was gone, Six had no one. She didn't want to be alone. She felt like Free had abandoned her and threw away all they had built over the years. It was like she didn't even know him. Britain was offering her a lifestyle of comfort, happiness, and wealth. He was offering her his heart. She knew that he had strong feelings for her. It poured out of him when he spoke to her, and she could feel it in his touch. The only thing that had ever stopped her from taking it all the way with Britain was Free. *Fuck him. He didn't appreciate what he had. Now I have to do what's right for me,* she thought.

Six looked up at Britain and replied, "I would say okay, but I'm not really in the state of mind to talk about us right now. I know I don't always act like it, but I'm really into you, Britain, and I'm lucky to have you in my life. If I didn't have you right now, I don't know where I would be. I need you to help me get through this. My father was my everything. He was the one person who was always here for me . . . no matter what, he always loved me."

Britain caressed her face and kissed the tip of her nose. "I'm here for you, Six. Know that no matter what happens here with us, I'm going to always make sure you're straight— believe that."

Free pulled up to Jones's house and discreetly wiped the tears that had accumulated in his eyes. *That's fucked up,* he thought as he got out of the car and pulled up his baggy denims before approaching the house. Jones had been good to Free and had accepted him with respect from the very first time they had met. His head was spinning when Big Lou delivered the news about Jones's murder, and he instantly began to worry about Six. He knew that he had gotten caught up and that they were beefing right now, but his girl needed him. He had never meant to hurt Six;

he hoped that Six could forgive him. He knew that their problems were not important right now. *I know she's hurting,* he thought. He saw firsthand just how close Six had been with her father, so he knew that she was going through it behind the murder. He just wanted to be there for her, but every time he called her phone he got her voice mail.

He strolled up the walkway and just as he was about to knock on the door, it opened. A white man answered, and they stared at each other in confusion. Free frowned when he read the tag on the man's green collar shirt.

*Cooper Cleaner and Recovery Service?* he thought.

"I'm looking for Six Jones," Free stated suspiciously.

"I'm sorry, sir. She isn't here, but we are supposed to deliver these belongings to her," the man informed him.

Free peeked inside the house. It was cleared out. He pulled out his phone and dialed Six's number, but got the same result—voice mail.

"Yo', my man, where are you delivering her stuff to?" Free asked as he rubbed the top of his head, something that he did when he was frustrated.

The worker looked down at the box in his hands and read the shipping label.

"Grosse Pointe Woods," he reported.

Free clenched his fists as his nostrils flared when he heard Britain's neighborhood. *She's moving in with that nigga,* he thought, enraged. "Fuck!" he yelled as he punched at the air in rage. He felt like he had just been punched in the gut. At this point, his life could not get much worse. *I have to talk to Six—the only reason she's giving that mu'fucka the time of day is because of that Sparkle bullshit,* Free thought. He trotted back to his car and started the engine. *I have to talk to her.*

# Chapter Sixteen

Six stood at the back of the church withering like an autumn leaf. She couldn't make herself walk down the aisle. She could see her father waiting for her up front. His casket sat among hundreds of white roses, her favorite flower, but she didn't have the strength to even put one foot in front of the other. Her eyes were blocked by the large Prada sunglasses she wore. She didn't want people to see her tired and weary eyes. It was as if her heart had died along with her father. She didn't want the world to judge her, so she hid behind the dark tint, wishing that she could keep them on forever. Six used all of her will to keep herself from crying. Her father wouldn't have wanted her whooping and hollering in front of the crowded room, so she contained her emotions, burying them so deep inside she was sure that she would be dealing with them for years to come.

Britain stood up from his seat in the front row. He had asked her if she wanted him to walk her down the aisle, but she had refused. She had assured him that she could handle it, but as he saw her stand frozen at the rear of the church, he disregarded her request and went to her aid.

"I'm right here," he whispered to her as he stood directly in front of her, blocking the crowd from seeing her face.

"Fuck all of these people, Six. You're here for Jones. You have to say good-bye to your father," Britain stated. "I'm right here with you, a'ight?"

Six stared straight ahead, never looking him in the eye. It was almost as if she were blind and had lost her way. She nodded and took a deep breath as she placed her hand on his.

Free's jaw clenched in anger as he watched Britain aid his woman. *Who the fuck this mu'fucka think he is?* he thought, enraged, as he looked at Britain and Six.

"Fuck is she doing, yo?" Free whispered to Big Lou.

"Just chill, fam . . . she's not in her right mind right now," Big Lou responded. Free had told him what had gone down with Sparkle and silently he knew that Free had made a bad move. It was already being said in the streets that Six belonged to Brick. Free picked the wrong time to fuck up. *From the looks of it, he pushed Six right into Brick's arms,* Lou thought.

"Yo, word is bond . . . she gon' fuck around and have me put that mu'fucka in the dirt. Straight up!" Free threatened, feeling his temperature rise. It killed him to see Britain by her side, because Free felt like that was his place, regardless of what they went through.

Leaning against Britain, Six was able to get down the aisle. When she saw her father lying there, the tears escaped her. She made sure that they were silent because she knew that people were waiting for her to act a fool. She would never make a mockery of her grief or of her father's life. She bent over when she arrived at the casket and kissed his forehead.

"You look good, Daddy," she whispered in his ear. One of her teardrops fell to his face as she stood up. Looking down at him as her own tear fell down his cheek, it looked as though he was crying with her. In her head she told herself that he was mourning his loss as well. By dying, he had been robbed of the chance to see his grandchildren or to walk his baby girl down the aisle. As that tear trailed his cheek, they cried together, saying their final good-bye. "I love you so much,

old man. . . . I love you forever. Wait for me,
okay, Daddy? Save my spot right next to you and
we'll smoke one together when I get there."

She adjusted his tie to make sure that he was
at his best and then she allowed Britain to escort
her to her seat. Before she sat down, she scanned
the crowd to see all of Jones's associates and old
friends. Her eyes met Free's, and she could see
the anger in his eyes. She knew him well, and she
could tell that he was boiling about seeing her
interacting so intimately with Britain. As they
stared at one another, her heart skipped a beat.
A guilty feeling overcame her as if she had been
caught cheating. She instantly released Britain's
hand, but then shook her head when she remembered the intimate kiss between Sparkle and
Free. *I don't owe him anything. Today is not
about him. It's about my daddy. He shouldn't
even be here,* she thought as she intertwined her
fingers with Britain's. Taking her seat, Six tried
to focus on the rest of the eulogy service as she
laid her father to rest.

When the service was over Six stood to leave.
Everyone came up to her expressing their condo-
lences and she accepted them graciously, but she
was desperate to get out of the church. She felt as
if she were suffocating.

"I need to get out of here," she whispered to
Britain as she gripped his sleeve.

He placed his hand on the small of her back, and they walked together toward the exit.

"I'm going to go to the restroom. I'll be right back," Britain said.

"I'll be waiting outside for you. I need some air," she responded.

When Six walked out of the building, Free stood on the church steps waiting for her.

"Six, I need to talk to you," he stated calmly while his eyes pleaded for her to hear him out.

Six ignored him as her heartbeat sped up and tears came to her eyes. She blinked them away and began to walk toward Britain's car.

"Oh, it's like that, ma. You just gon' pass me by," Free stated coldly. He followed her and grabbed her arm to make her face him. "Six, I'm sorry. Just give a minute to explain what went down. It didn't mean shit to me," he stated. "I love you, Six. You've got to come home."

"Is there a problem?" Britain interrupted, suddenly appearing behind Free.

Free looked over his shoulder and scrunched his face. "I don't know, my nigga. *Is* there a problem?" Free countered as he took a defensive stance, placing his hands on his belt for easy access to his pistol. There wasn't a place in the world where he didn't go strapped, and Six knew this so she quickly intervened.

"Britain, let's just go," she said in exasperation. She was tired and weak. All of this was too much for her to deal with on the same day that she was burying her father.

"Let's go?" Free asked. "So it's like that? You just gon' leave with this nigga?" He grabbed her arm, and Britain quickly removed Free's hand, causing Free's to shoot through the roof.

"Yo, my man . . . you need to back the fuck up," Britain stated without raising his voice, but with enough authority to establish dominance over the situation. Free did not know it, but Britain was strapped as well and had three of his goons surrounding the church. . . . He never left home without them.

"No, you need to back the fuck up, nigga! Way up! You sniffing around the wrong tree. This here is my bitch," Free stated through clenched teeth.

"Was your bitch," Britain replied calmly. He leaned into Free's ear and continued, "Now she's my bitch, and once she fuck with Brick, ain't no sliding back. . . . I upgraded that. Stickup money can't afford that no more."

Free and Britain both went into their waistlines, but before they could pop off, Six stepped in between the altercation.

"Stop! What the fuck? This is my daddy's funeral!" She turned to Free and went off, letting out all of her anger on him. "You didn't even say one word about him . . . all this time you've been out here talking about you, Free. What about me? What about what I lost? My father's gone, and all you came here to do is fight with Britain." She shook her head in disgust as she walked away crying on Britain's shoulder.

"You choosing him? After everything, Six— that's who you choose?" Free yelled.

Six stopped dead in her tracks and stalked back over to where Free was standing. She pushed him as she cried hysterically.

"You chose, Free! You made the decision for me when you fucked with Sparkle," Six replied.

"Six, let's go," Britain called, tired of the circus as he reached out his hand. Free put his hands on his head as he watched the woman he loved walk away with the man he hated. Tears were in his eyes, but he didn't let them fall.

"Yo, Free!" he heard Big Lou call as he pulled up the car. "It's over, fam—let's get out of here. Let her cool down."

Free walked to the car and collapsed in the passenger seat. "She chose him, fam," he whispered in disbelief as Big Lou pulled away from the church.

\*\*\*

"Come on, Daddy, let me make you feel better," Sparkle cooed seductively as put on a little freak show, trying to lure in her prey.

Free stood in front of her shirtless with a pint of Rémy in his hands. His eyes were low, and the haze from a rolled blunt fogged the room. Free had been intoxicated from the time he left Jones's funeral. It was the way he dealt with his heartache over losing Six. He hit the last of the Rémy and blazed his blunt before climbing into the bed with Sparkle.

Sparkle had come over to see Free. Hood gossip traveled fast, and she had heard about the blowup that had occurred at the funeral. She knew that now was her chance to hook Free. She had been eyeing him ever since Six had introduced her. Free always seemed so loyal to Six, until recent events drove them apart. She was a seductress, and she was well aware that the best time to weasel her way into Free's heart was while he was feeling the twinge of loneliness from losing Six.

Free was past the point of intoxication as he climbed into bed with Sparkle. She tried to kiss his lips, but he turned his head. Kissing was a personal act; he simply wanted to sex his frustrations away. Sparkle winced from the size of him as he entered her.

"Ooh, Free," she moaned as he put his thing down on her. He had to admit being inside of Sparkle felt like heaven. He pounded into her as he took out his misery on her, sexing her hard, just the way she liked it. Her screams of passion turned him on as he pulled out and turned her around to hit it from a new position.

She laid her breasts against the bed while her behind enticed him. The tattoo of a dripping cherry looked good enough to eat. He hesitated for a moment as he thought of Six. She had hurt him. His pride was wounded, and his gut felt like it had been ripped out of him. He was lovesick without her because he knew that she was not coming back.

Sparkle sensed his hesitation and jiggled her juicy behind. "Come on, Free. Six forgot about you a long time ago. You should hear how she talks about Britain on the phone. You're not even on her radar anymore," she said, pulling lies out of her bag of tricks.

Free grabbed his manhood and pushed Sparkle's head into the pillows to shut her up. He had never felt so incomplete. Six was his world, and without her, his heart was rotting inside his chest. He went inside of Sparkle and began to stroke her from behind. As she cried out in ecstasy, a single tear slid down Free's cheek.

\*\*\*

Six wiped the tears from her eyes as she lay in the guest room of Britain's home, staring at the ceiling. *How did my life come to this?* she asked. She had lost so much in such a short amount of time. The two men who she valued more than gold were now gone from her life. She felt as if she had been stripped naked in a room of crowded people. Surprisingly, Britain was the shining light around the dark cloud. *He's so good to me,* Six thought. *I can't believe I ever even considered setting him up. He doesn't deserve that.* She looked at all of the boxes that were scattered around the room. Her father's possessions lay inside of them. She didn't have the courage to sort them out yet. She was too vulnerable. She wanted to give herself time to heal before she began going through his things.

As she tossed and turned in the satin sheets, she hit the bed in aggravation. She couldn't get comfortable. Thoughts of Free plagued her, and visions of her father haunted her. The sting of Free's betrayal was just as hurtful as the kiss of death. He had cheated on her before, but to get involved with her best friend meant that Free had no limits. He had no morals in her eyes. *Someone who loves you wouldn't do that,* she reasoned. She never knew that a pain so great existed before now. She listened to the still of the night and suddenly the thought of being alone terrified her. *I wonder if Britain's still awake,* she thought.

She threw the covers off her body and got out of bed. Her feet against the cold tile floor caused goose bumps to form on her bare arms. The Victoria's Secret camisole was too thin to keep her warm, and she rubbed herself as she ventured out of the room. She tiptoed down the hall and put her ear to Britain's door. All she heard was silence. She turned to go back to her room but stopped and shook her head. *There's nothing wrong with being with him. . . . He cares about you. You don't belong to Free anymore. Britain will take care of you,* she coached herself as she took a deep breath then opened the door to step inside.

His room smelled like vanilla, and she could see him breathing slightly as she crossed the room. She pulled back his covers, rousing him from his sleep. "What's wron—?"

Before he could get the question out of his mouth, Six's tongue was down his throat. He put his hands up in defense at first because she caught him off guard. He had not expected this. Six kissed him fervently as tears flowed down her face. Both of her hands held his face, and she squeezed her eyes closed while her heart beat out of her chest. Britain wrapped his arms around her body, both of them panting as their lips never parted while they undressed each other. Her head fell back in ecstasy as Britain palmed one of her breasts and took her nipple into his mouth. They didn't speak, but the sounds of their love-making conquered the room when he slid his manhood inside of her. The girth of his tool took her breath away as it filled her up, exploring depths of her that she did not know existed.

"Hmm," he moaned.

"Uhh," she whined in reply as they moved to a slow beat, matching each other stroke by stroke. She was on top, but Britain controlled the situation as their bodies became one. He had waited a long time for Six, and the anticipation that built up to this one moment made the episode that much more explosive. It was the best sex that either of them had ever had. Six finally felt free. She had been torn between two men for the past few months and finally she was letting go. She was allowing herself to fully experience a relationship with Britain. As they sexed, the fit between them was so perfect that her pussy exploded with every thrust he gave her. He reached up and grabbed her breasts as she rode him, allowing her thighs to make tiny circles as her ass bounced up and down. The ride was so smooth that Britain's toes curled. Six sped up and thrust harder simultaneously when she felt her clitoris swell.

"Aghh!" she screamed as her love came down. She had never been a squirter before, but with Britain, her juices shot out all over his stomach. As she got off of him, Six knew that she wasn't done just yet. She was going to give him 100 percent of her. She lay on top of him, her juicy pussy in his face and her head near his manhood. Without hesitation, she took him into her mouth.

"Ohh, shit," he whispered. He placed his hands on her ass and spread her cheeks as he ate her pussy. The smell of her was so sweet that it made his dick harder. She wrapped her lips around his tip and molested his dick with her tongue as she rode his face. Britain wasn't shy with her. He hadn't waited this long to fuck her just to half step. He stuck his tongue in her ass and thrust his hips to feed her his entire nine inches.

Six hummed in rapture as he alternated between sucking her hole and nibbling on her clit. Meanwhile, she gave him head like a pro. She knew that he was about to nut because his grip on her ass grew tighter and tighter. She rotated her hips on his face until finally they both exploded. Six surprised herself when she didn't pull away. She let him cum in her mouth and swallowed every drop of his seed and then licked him clean. Without saying a word she got out of bed.

"Where you going?" he asked.

She turned around with tears in her eyes and beckoned him with her finger. "We're going to take a shower," she replied.

Britain followed Six into the bathroom and their shower turned into round two as he pinned her against the ceramic tiled wall and fucked her from behind. She cried the entire time—not because she was unsure, but because she could feel how much he loved her. Britain did not know it, but with each tender kiss and every stroke he relieved her of some of her pain. They sexed each other for hours and when the sun began to rise, they found themselves sitting on his balcony, wrapped in the sheets. Six leaned against him, her back against his chest as he kissed her repeatedly while rubbing her hair soothingly.

"I think I love you, Britain," she whispered as she kissed his hand. She had only spoken those words to two people in her entire lifetime: her father and Free. She had never even told her mother that she loved her. Now she was letting her father rest and retiring her emotions for

Free. She didn't know that Free had done the same thing—made love to someone else to distract his mind and heart from her.

"I love you too, ma," he replied. "I know your heart is broken, but let me heal you. I'm not on no wedding-bell shit. I just want to have you as my own. Fuck another nigga and fuck another bitch—just me and you, Six. That's what I want us to be about. If you can give me that, I can give you the world."

She turned to face him and kissed his lips. "I can give you that. I'm here with you."


After a full night of nonstop sex, Six didn't awaken until four o'clock the next day. Her pussy throbbed, and she shook her head in disbelief as she recalled all of the things that Britain had done to her body the night before. She got up to find him, but he was nowhere to be found. *Oh, well, I might as well use this time wisely,* she thought as she went into the guest room where her father's things were stored.

As she unpacked each box, she reminisced and remembered all of the things she loved about her father. She laughed as she looked at old photo albums and surprisingly not a tear fell from her eyes as she decided what she would

keep and what would go. She came across her father' favorite Detroit Pistons sweatshirt. He had
purchased it years ago when he had taken her to
a game at the Palace. She inhaled his scent as she
put it to her nose. Then she slipped it over her
head, feeling closer to him just from the simple
gesture. It took her two hours to finish, but she
felt like a weight had been lifted off her shoulders when she completed the task. Suddenly,
her cell phone rang loudly and she hopped up to
answer it, thinking that it was Britain.

*Where is he?* she thought as she picked up her
phone. Free's name popped up on the caller ID.
She closed her eyes as her heart throbbed pain-
fully. *I can't do this with you, Free. I have to let
you go,* she thought as hung up on him. Directly
afterward she called her phone company and got
her number changed. That part of her life was
over and she didn't need Free calling her, trying
to lure her back into his arms. He had disrespected her, and she was beyond done. *Sparkle
and Free deserve one another,* she thought mis-
erably. *I hope he enjoys the scar I put on that
bitch face.*

"Six!" she heard Britain call out. The house
was so large that his voice echoed off the walls.

She came down the steps and ran into his
arms. "I missed you—where have you been all

day?" she said. "You tired of me already?" she asked as she hit him playfully.

He smacked her on the behind and kissed her cheek. "Never that," he replied. All of a sudden a beeping sound came from outside.

"What is that?" she asked as she went to the window. "What the fuck?" she yelled. "There's a tow truck outside. This nigga is getting ready to tow my car." She ran outside and raced down the courthouse-style steps. "What are you doing?"

"I'm sorry, miss. The owner of this house paid me to get rid of this car," he stated.

Six turned back to Britain and looked at him in confusion. He nodded toward the entrance, and she turned to see what he was looking at. One of his goons was driving a car onto the property: a silver 2010 E-Class Mercedes-Benz with a turquoise ribbon. He stopped right in front of her.

"My woman doesn't ride in a car that another nigga bought for her, especially an Audi. My bitch push Benzes," he whispered in her ear.

She jumped up on him, wrapping her legs around his waist in excitement.

"I take it I did good?" he asked with a laugh.

"Nigga, you did great! I love it!" she exclaimed.

"This is just the beginning," he said, kissing her cheek.

As Six checked out the features in her new car, she couldn't help but think about what she was leaving behind. Free had done all of the same things for her in the beginning of their relationship. Trips, cars, and clothes were simply a day in the life. Time changed them, however, and distrust tore them apart. She couldn't help but wonder if she was setting herself up again for the exact same failure. She wanted a man who she knew would never hurt her, but in matters of the heart, there are no guarantees. As she stared up at Britain, she saw him smile her way as he spoke to his worker who had delivered the car for him. *Just take a chance,* she thought as she smiled back. *Just move on with your life and be happy. He can give you happiness,* she thought.

# Chapter Seventeen

Free looked over at Sparkle and couldn't stand the sight of her. It had been two months since Six had caught them fooling around, and he hadn't spoken to Six since her father's funeral. Six had no kick it for Free.

*Damn,* he thought as he looked at Sparkle's belly, knowing that in a month or two she would be showing. She was two months pregnant with his baby, and he had to live with the bad choice he had made. Free and Sparkle had been robbing niggas for the past two months nonstop. There were no boundaries for who they would hit. They had less than $100,000 dollars, which wasn't nearly enough to pay back Claude.

"Okay, look, Sparkle. We have to try to hit niggas every night," Free said coaching her and regretting the fact that he had started sleeping with her after the big incident with Six.

"Damn, Free. You act like you my pimp a' something. I am carrying your child, and you don't even

care. You just throwing me to the wolves! We are
about to start a family," she said as she rubbed her
stomach.

Free clenched his teeth and couldn't understand how he had let this thing go so far. Six
had gotten her number changed, and every time
he went over to Jones's house, she was always
gone. His heart was broken, and extreme guilt
burdened him. Free wasn't going to tell Sparkle
his plan, which was to force her to get an abor-
tion just before the three-month mark of the
pregnancy. He also knew that Sparkle would
probably not want to help him rob hustlers once
he exposed his ulterior motives to her. He was
just using her for what he needed, and he would
simply kick her to the curb and pursue Six after
he got his money from the robbing game.

"We are going to be a family," Free lied as he
reached over and stroked her hair, giving her
a big smile. Sparkle blushed as she looked into
Free's eyes, thinking that her dream had finally
come true. Little did she know she was just a
pawn in Free's mental chess game. Free felt his
phone vibrate and quickly reached for it, hoping
it was Six. But he was disappointed when he saw
Big Lou on the caller ID.

"What's up, fam?" Free asked as he put his
phone to his ear. Big Lou began to give him the

rundown on a potential victim who sold major weed on the east side of Detroit. All the while, Sparkle had leaned over and pulled Free's dick out, sucking it while it was soft and eventually making it rock-hard within seconds.

Free listened closely to Big Lou while at the same time, enjoying Sparkle's best talent. She moaned while licking him like a lollipop. Free was so consumed in getting head while trying to listen to Lou that he didn't notice the tinted truck that had been following him for the past two blocks.

The tinted truck sped up and crept alongside of Free as they both approached a stoplight. The truck's passenger-side window rolled down, exposing the masked gunman. Free never saw it coming as he threw his head back, enjoying the blow job and feeling himself about to explode in Sparkle's jaws.

The masked man slowly pulled out an AK-47 assault rifle as he leaned half of his body out of the window. One second later, bullets flew rapidly out of the gun and into Free's car.

The thundering sounds of shattering glass and bullets thumping the car's metal rang out. Glass flew inside of the car along with bullets as Free ducked down trying to dodge death. Sparkle rose from Free's crotch and a single bullet struck her in her temple, killing her instantly. Her blood splattered all over the passenger-side window as she lay slumped with her eyes wide open.

Free quickly hit the gas while still ducked down. He caught two bullets to his shoulder as he wildly drove the car trying to escape the assassination attempt. He violently crashed into a telephone pole, crushing his entire front end. His air bags burst, hitting him in the face and knocking him unconscious because of its brute force. The tinted truck sped away down the street, tires screeching, leaving Free for dead.

# Chapter Eighteen

"Britain! We're going to be late!" Six yelled as she dusted a piece of lint off of her cream-colored Donna Karan pant suit.

Britain took his time as he inserted his cuff links and replied, "I can't be late, ma—I own the place."

It was a routine they did every Sunday. Britain, Six, and all of the people closest to him in his operation met at his restaurant to have breakfast. It kept them close and established that they were like family. Today was special for Brick, however. Two months had passed since Six had moved in with him, and life for him could not get any better. For the first time since his father was killed, Britain felt whole. Six brought a joy to his life that fulfilled, him and today in front of all of the people he held dear, he was going to ask her to be his wife.

He grabbed her coat out of the closet and held it out for her so that she could ease into it, then they took off.

When they arrived in the restaurant, they were both greeted with welcome arms and Six took her seat next to Britain at the head of the table. She suddenly felt funny. There was something in the air that made chills run up and down her spine. She shook the feeling off as they began to converse and eat their breakfast. Just looking at Six one would be able to tell that she had the best of everything. The diamond rocks in her ear, expensive threads on her body, and the spa-treated glow that graced her skin told any onlookers that she was royalty. Britain had completely remodeled her. Six had always been a ten in the looks department, but now she was the total package. She was a lady—the armpiece of a hustler, and the woman that every chick in the hood wanted to be.

As Britain watched Six interact with his crew, he realized that he was making the right decision. He had been through many women, and none of them were even comparable to Six. She had given him the best two months of his life. She wasn't a pushover by far and would argue him down tooth and nail just to get her point across, but Britain liked her strong will. He respected it because he recognized where it came from. She was a direct reflection of her father and a perfect representation of what he wanted his future child's mother to be. Most people would think that he was moving way too fast, but Britain knew time was of the essence. Tomorrow was not promised in the lifestyle he was leading, so he was going after what he wanted today.

Britain tapped his fork against his glass to get everyone's attention and just as he was about to speak, Big Lou barged into the restaurant. He stormed over to the table.

"Six!" Big Lou called out.

Britain nodded and instantly two members of his crew stood up and grabbed Big Lou's arms, stopping him in his tracks. Big Lou snatched his arms out of their hold. "Six, I got to talk to you!" he stated urgently.

Six felt torn between her current life and her past one. She looked over at Britain who sat back in his seat calmly, but the fire in his eyes told a different story. He began to stand, but Six grabbed his hand. "No, baby, I've got it—just give me a minute, okay?" she asked, her perfectly arched eyebrows begging him to be cool.

Britain's nostrils flared, but he nodded and leaned over to whisper in her ear. "Tell that mu'fucka next time he comes in here to show some respect. Handle your business, ma. Nod your head if you need me, beautiful." He kissed the side of her cheek and she stood.

Six rushed to Big Lou and quickly ushered him outside.

"What are you thinking running in here like that?" she asked, chastising her old friend. "What do you want, Lou? Did Free send you here? Because I don't have shit to say to him—"

"He's in the hospital, Six," Big Lou interrupted as he put his hand on top of his head.

Her hard visage instantly faded away as worry filled her eyes. The blood drained from her face, and her heart throbbed. "What?" she stated.

"He got shot!" Big Lou said. "He don't have no family, Six. You're his family. I know y'all not like that no more, but I had to come tell you. If it's his time to go, I know he would want to see your face, nah'mean?"

Six looked back inside and saw Britain staring at her. Tears came to her eyes as the sidewalk felt like it was spinning beneath her feet. She didn't know what to do. Stay or leave? Leave or stay? It was a simple question with a complex answer. Whatever she chose to do after that moment would undoubtedly have consequences.

"Where is he?" she asked.

"He's at Henry Ford Hospital—come on, I'll take you," Big Lou stated as he ran to his car that was parked curbside.

***

Six took off behind him and hopped into the car. *Please let him be okay,* she thought as she watched the cold city of Detroit fly.

Britain lowered his head and took a deep breath as the entire table grew silent. He knew that they were waiting on him to say something. He opened the ring box and looked at the princess-cut stone he had chosen for Six. His temple throbbed because he already knew that she was going somewhere to meet Free. He recognized Big Lou as Free's people and was disappointed that she had chosen to leave without letting him know what was what. He closed the velvet box and placed the ring in his inside jacket pocket.

"Let's eat," he said, not revealing his mood in his tone. Britain looked at his Rolex and noticed that it was only ten o'clock. His breakfast ritual usually didn't end until around noon and then he chopped it up with his workers until around four in the afternoon, so he would have to wait until then to contact Six. He wasn't going to chase behind her, but she did have some explaining to do.

Six rushed into the hospital and waited anxiously as Big Lou spoke with the nurses. Free was still in surgery, and no one would tell them anything so all they could do was wait. Six tortured herself as she thought of how much time had passed them by. She hadn't seen or heard from Free in eight weeks. She had not even thought to pick up the phone and call him.

"I was so stupid," she whispered. She turned to look at Big Lou. "What if he dies, Lou? What if I never get the chance to tell him I'm sorry?"

"Don't talk like that, sis. He'll pull through," Lou stated aloud in an attempt to be supportive.

Six put her face in her hands and closed her eyes as she tried to calm down. Feelings that she thought she had buried for Free began to come back. At that point she didn't give a damn about Sparkle and Free, all she wanted was to hear him say her name again. She wanted Free to live more than anything she had ever wanted in her life. As her heart beat out of her chest, she realized that she still loved him, but her emotions confused her because she was positive that she cared for Britain as well.

Finally, a doctor emerged from behind the double doors and she stood nervously. "How is he?" she asked. "Can I see him?"

"He is stable and in very good condition. He was shot in his arm, but the bullet completely severed his main artery. We repaired the artery and removed the bullet, but he lost a substantial amount of blood. He will be extremely weak for a few weeks. We'd like to keep him for observation."

Six didn't hear anything past the part where the doctor told her Free was alive. "Can I see him?" she asked, becoming emotional.

The doctor nodded and led Six and Big Lou to Free's room.

As soon as Six saw Free, the floodgates opened and she couldn't plug them no matter how hard she tried. She pulled a chair near his bedside.

"I'm here, Free—I'm so sorry," she stated as she kissed his lips.

"I love you, Six," he said in a groggy tone as he opened his eyes. It felt as if his eyelids weighed a thousand pounds, but he fought to open them anyway. He could hear Six's voice in his ear, now all he wanted to do was see her face.

"I love you, too," she whispered as she held his hand and sat beside him.

The doctor left the room, and Six turned to Big Lou. "I should have never left him. This is all my fault. If I had just gotten the money so that Free could pay the Russians, none of this would have ever happened."

"This ain't on you," Big Lou stated. "I got something else to tell you. I didn't want to tell you before because I wasn't sure if you would come if you knew."

"What?" she asked.

"Sparkle was in the car with Free when it got lit up. She's dead," Big Lou stated.

Six instantly formed questions in her mind. *What were they doing together? Why did Free have to get involved with my best friend?* She wanted so badly to say something, but she knew that none of that really mattered. Those were her own insecurities, and Free didn't have the strength to argue or fight. She held her tongue and simply replied, "Thanks for telling me, Lou."

As she looked back down at Free, she knew that he was her soul mate. Many people may call her a fool, but sometimes destiny is too strong to fight. She loved Free and, no, he wasn't perfect, but he needed her, and she would be fake to turn her back on him.

"I have to go pay the Russians," she said. Free had fallen back to sleep, and she turned to Big Lou. "Do you know where I can find Claude?" she asked.

Big Lou nodded. "How are you going to get the money?"

She sighed as she thought of what she was about to do. She was going to hurt the man who loved her in order to save Free. Britain was so good to her, and she wished that it did not have to come to this, but she did not see any other way. Maybe if she and Britain had not reunited under such corrupt circumstances they would have had a chance, but from the beginning, she was his enemy. Their relationship would never last because eventually their rocky foundation would crumble. She cared deeply for him, but she was Free's. They had hit many bumps in the road, but in the end, they always came back to one another. Unfortunately for Britain, he had gotten caught in the drama, and she was going to break his heart. "I'm going to stick to the plan and hit Britain's safe," she replied.

"You sure you can pull it off?" Big Lou asked.

"Of course, I can. I'm his wifey—I've had access to everything for the past two months," she revealed.

Six looked at the clock and saw that it was only two P.M. *I have to get back to the house before Britain gets there.* She wanted to be in and out like a robbery. She would leave everything that he had ever purchased for her, but she didn't have a choice but to empty out his safe. If she didn't, then she was pretty sure that the Russians would come back and this time they wouldn't miss.

# Chapter Nineteen

Six hurried as she threw the stacks of money in her two large Gucci bags. The only thing on her mind was getting the money for Free before Britain returned from the Sunday dinner. It broke her heart thinking about taking the money from Britain's safe after he had given her his trust. Although she and Free had been through their differences over the past two months, her loyalty was with him. She still loved him and never wanted to see harm come his way. *I have to pay those Russians before they come and finish Free off,* she thought as water began to form in her eyes.

It took Free being shot for her to realize how much she needed and loved him. Although Britain treated her like a queen and spoiled her, Free was her man no matter what. They had a connection that was everlasting. She planned on telling Britain the truth after she paid Free's debt with the Russians.

Six filled each bag to its capacity and zipped them both up. She didn't know how much was in the bags, but she figured that it was more than enough; being that it was all Benjamin Franklins.

Six headed down the stairs to meet Lou, who was waiting at the hospital for her. Just as she hit the bottom step, she heard keys jingling in the door. "Fuck," she whispered as Britain was coming in. Six froze in fear, not knowing what to say to him. She had a bag full of his money and was caught red-handed. Britain stepped in calmly and noticed Six's nervous demeanor as she stood still, her guilty eyes resembling a deer caught in headlights.

"Six, what's going on?" Britain asked in concern as he closed the door behind him. "I have been calling you nonstop. You just rushed out of the restaurant without putting me up on game," he said as he walked over to her, cradled her cheek, and pecked her on the forehead. "What's in the bags? You going somewhere?" he asked as his facial expression changed, displaying his puzzlement. He was unsure of what was going on. He took a step back and glanced at the bag and noticed stacks of money through the unzipped portion. "What's in the bag?" he asked again, but this time with more authority and through clenched teeth as he stared at the money-filled bags suspiciously.

"Nothing, it's just a couple pieces," Six lied as her heart began to thump rapidly and her hands began to sweat. Britain calmly grabbed one of the bags out of her hand and opened it up. When he found out his suspicions were right, it broke his heart. He handed the bag back to Six and took another step back. Then he chuckled, trying to laugh off his broken heart instead of becoming angry.

"Nothing, huh? That's a whole lot of nothing in that bag," he stated as he leaned against the wall and slyly put his hands in his designer slacks.

"Look, I can explain," Six said as she dropped the bags and started to walk toward him. "Britain, I—" before Six could begin her next sentence Britain raised his hand to stop her from approaching and calmly responded.

"That's for Free, huh?" he asked, already knowing what the deal was. He couldn't believe that Six would betray him like she had. Six was at a loss for words and didn't know how to respond. A tear slid down her cheek as she saw the pain in Britain's eyes.

"You don't have to explain. You can have all of what's in that safe. There's more where that came from, believe me. But before you leave, do me one favor," Britain said just before he pulled out his car keys and walked toward the door. "Make sure you leave the house key on the table and take your shit with you." Britain exited the house, leaving Six standing there alone and dumbfounded.

"Britain! Wait!" she yelled as she looked at the door in disbelief. "Damn," she yelled as she fell to her knees. Moments later, she heard the screeching of Britain's car and she understood that they would never be the same. Their relationship had run its course. Although she truly cared for him, the relationship had been built on a lie, and now that the truth had surfaced, there was no turning back. She knew that she would have to deal with Britain later, but right now, she worried about Free's safety.

Six took one last look around her—the magnificent place that had been her temporary safe haven then felt the necklace on her neck. She removed the expensive diamond, feeling as if she no longer deserved to wear it. The picture of her with Britain and his father caught her eye. She kissed her fingers and placed a kiss on the frame. *Good-bye Britain,* she thought somberly. Then she picked up the bags full of money and headed to the hospital so Big Lou could take her to the man responsible for almost ending Free's life.

Lou drove Six to the bar establishment that Claude owned and kept offering to take the money, but Six refused.

"These mu'fuckas ain't playing, Big Lou. No telling what they will do to you if you go inside. Obviously they don't care about getting their money anymore, because they tried to kill Free. You got to let me do this," she said as Lou parked a couple buildings down from the bar.

"Okay, I will be right back," Six said as she took the bags from the backseat. Lou grabbed her hand just before she got out of the car and pulled out a small gun.

"Here, take this," he instructed. "I'll be right out here waiting on you, sis."

Six took the gun and concealed it in her Coach boot just before she headed to the establishment.

When Six walked through the doors, a bartender yelled, "We're closed, sweetheart," as he wiped off the bar top. A couple of men were toward the back at a table playing cards, and Six scoped the entire scene before responding.

"I'm here to see Claude," she said loudly so everyone in the room could hear her clearly. "I'm here about Free," Six said smugly as she looked at the bartender square in the eyes.

"You're Alfree's woman, huh? That son a' bitch sent his woman to do his dirty work," he said jokingly as he glanced back at the guys in the corner of the room. The bartender looked down at the bags and knew that she was here to pay a debt. He hopped over the counter and stood right in front of Six. Six showed no fear as she looked up at the man and didn't budge. "Raise your arms."

"Sure," Six said as she followed the orders, hoping that he wouldn't check her boot. The man patted her down but didn't go near the boot where the gun was hidden.

"She's clean!" he yelled as he stepped to the side to let Six go toward the back. Six walked with a model's precision across the floor, the high heels of her boots clicking the hardwood floor with every step. "Here is your money. Call your goons off," she said as she dropped the bag on the table, interrupting their card game.

"Whoa, whoa," Claude said as he threw both of his hands up and sat back in his seat. "No hello? How ya doing or nothing?" he asked sarcastically as he smiled and looked down at the bags in front of him. He then opened up the bags and saw the stacks of money.

"Is Free's debt settled now or what?' Six asked as she put both of her hands on her hips and tapped the floor with her right foot. Claude smiled and zipped the bag back up.

"As much as I want to take this money, I can't, sweetheart," Claude responded.

"What? But it's all there. Maybe even more," Six pleaded.

"His debt was taken care of months ago. I don't have any beef with Alfree," Claude stated.

"What?" Six asked as she frowned up in confusion.

"What, you got wax in ya ears, sweetheart? I don't have a beef with Free anymore. His debt has been paid," Claude repeated.

"So why did you try to kill him?" Six asked, trying to put the pieces of the puzzle together.

"Kill him? I had nothing to do with that. Some guy came in and dropped three hundred large right in my lap. Boom," Claude said, emphasizing how the man dropped the money on the table. "And he said that Free's debt had just been paid. I think he said his name was . . . Brick."

Lou couldn't understand why Six come back out with the money in her hands. She wouldn't respond to him, and she looked like she was in deep thought. They cruised the streets en route back to the hospital.

"Are you going to tell me what's going on or what, Six? Why didn't he take the money?" Lou asked as he kept his eyes on the road.

"Lou, hold on, I have to figure some shit out," Six said as she put her finger up and thought about the recent events. *Britain paid off Free's debt? Why? Did he know the real reason I initially got at him? Did he try to kill Free? He couldn't have. Or could he? I'm so fucking confused,* Six thought as she buried her face in her hands. So many unanswered questions popped in her head.

Lou began to check his mirror, noticing a tinted truck that had been following them for a couple of blocks. He reached up and positioned the mirror to get a better angle on the vehicle behind them.

"What the fuck?" Lou said under his breath after he hit a quick right and the truck did just the same. Six raised her head to see what was going on.

"What's up, Lou?" she asked as she noticed him repeatedly look in his rearview and speed up the car.

"I think someone is following us," Lou said as he hit another corner, but this time it was with more speed, causing the tires to squeal. "Put on your seat belt, sis," Lou said as he pushed her chest back to brace her. He then reached under his seat and pulled out chrome 9 mm and set it on his lap, already locked and loaded.

Six buckled her seat belt, and Lou gunned it. The torque of the Dodge Charger's hemi engine roared and within five seconds Lou was at sixty-five miles per hour, racing down Woodward Avenue. The tinted truck was right on their tail.

"Who the fuck is that?" Six screamed as she turned around and watched the truck edge near them and then crash into their back, rear-ending them. Both of their bodies jerked from the much-larger truck hitting them. Go! Go!" Six yelled as she feared for her life.

The tinted truck rear-ended them again, but this time with more force, causing Lou's back window to shatter. His car temporarily spun out of control, and they came to a screeching halt in the middle of the vacant street.

Lou had enough of the cat-and-mouse game. He looked in the rearview and saw that the truck stopped also. It was just about fifty yards away from them and the driver was revving the engine, making the truck shake. Lou jumped out with his gun in hand and began firing while walking to-ward the truck. The truck spun around and sped off after a couple of hollow tips began to hit the exterior. Lou emptied the clip until the truck was out of sight. He returned to his truck breathing heavily.

"Who in the hell was that?" Six said as she rose from the crouching position she was in.

"I wish I could tell you. Somebody wants us dead. Let's hurry up and get to Free. Gotta get the fuck up outta here," Lou said just before he pulled off. The mystery person behind the wheel was trying to kill them, and Six knew that whoever it was probably was the same person who had killed Sparkle and shot Free. Six was boggled, and the only thing on her mind was getting to Free and leaving the city. She wasn't turning back.

*Three Weeks Later*

Six nursed Free back to health and stayed with him every day in physical therapy, trying to get his motor skills back in his arm. She decided to tell the nurse to list Free under an alias, just in case the person who tried to kill him came back to finish the job.

Lou attended Sparkle's funeral on Free's behalf. Her memorial service was held a week after she was murdered and come to find out she wasn't pregnant at the time of her death. She put on a front just to try to get Free as her own. Free was shocked at the news and decided not to ever tell Six about what they had going on. He felt that what she didn't know would not hurt her.

Eventually Free was walking out of the hospital and upset that he had been shot, but happy to have Six back again.

"Thanks, baby," Free said as she helped him into Lou's car. Free looked at Six and vowed never to part from his woman again. *That girl is my soul mate*, he thought as he felt a sharp pain shoot up his arm. He grimaced as he strapped on his seat belt and Six closed the passenger door for him. Lou drove, and Six got in the backseat.

"I glad you home, boy," Lou said as he playfully hit Free upside his head. He then started up the car, preparing to leave the hospital parking lot.

"Yeah, but I got to get to the money now. I want to pay them Russians and be done with it. I could have died that night. We not strong enough to go to war with the mu'fuckas, so I just got to pay them," Free said as the burdens of life began to weigh down on him. The frustration was written all over his face. Lou smiled as he looked back at Six, who was in the backseat.

"You didn't tell him, sis?" Lou asked her.

"Oh, yeah. That debt is paid. I got a surprise for you too," Six said excitedly to Free.

"The debt is paid? What?" Free asked as he tried to maneuver his body to turn around. Before he knew it, Six reached over and put a heavy duffel bag in his lap.

"What's this?" Free asked as he looked down at the Gucci bag.

"Open it and see," Six said as she rubbed his shoulders to comfort him. Free did as he was told and when he opened the bag, he couldn't help but to smile. *My down-ass bitch*, he thought as the eyes of Benjamin Franklin stared up at him. Through all the heartache, Six still came through for him and followed through with the plan to rob Britain.

"That's about $200,000 dollars in there. I got another bag back here that has about $75,000," Six said proudly as she continued to rub her man.

"I guess the plan worked," Free said as he felt so relieved.

"Yeah, baby! You know I never forgot whose side I was on, even though you almost forgot whose side you were on," Six responded as she thought about Britain. Although she had just told Free that she was sure she was on the right side, at one point she almost forgot and had indeed fallen for Britain. She had suspicions that he was the one who tried to kill Free, but she decided to let it go and start over with Free.

"Oh, yeah, Lou, I didn't forget about you," she said as she grabbed $75,000 dollars that she had already put in a paper bag for him. She tossed that into his lap, and he smiled like a kid in a candy store.

"That's what I'm talking about, sis. Hold yo' bro down," Lou said as he flipped through the bills.

"That's my baby!" Free yelled as he picked up a stack of bills and kissed it. Free wanted to ask about Britain, but he just wanted to move forward and begin his life with Six. "No more worries," he whispered.

"No more worries," Six confirmed as she sat back in her seat as Lou pulled off.


Six wore a comfortable jogging suit as she directed the movers in and out of her house. She and Free were finally moving out of Detroit to start a life without malice and the treachery that the inner city of Detroit had to offer. They used the money that she had taken from Britain to put a down payment on a home in Auburn Hills, a suburban area away from Detroit.

"Lou, get yo' big ass in here and pick up a box!" Six yelled jokingly as Lou had his head in their refrigerator.

"That's what you paying them for," Lou said as he walked out with a hoagie sandwich in his hand. "Where is Free?" he asked as he walked toward Six.

"I think he's outside," Six answered as she bent down and began taping up some of the moving boxes.

Free stood outside eyeing the tinted truck that was parked in the middle of the street. He felt something was odd, and he stared at the vehicle closely. Although Free had a sling on his arm, he raised up his shirt, displaying his gun that was tucked in his waist and threw one hand up as if he was inviting the person to get at him. The car immediately sped off, leaving Free standing there with his hand up. Once the car got out of sight, Free waved his hand in dismissal.

"Coward-ass nigga," he whispered as he turned around and returned inside the house.

"Big Lou, you strapped?" Free asked as he walked in the door, just to make sure they were ready for whatever.

"You *knoooow* it," Lou said in a melodic tone as he patted his waist.

"Why, what's up?" Six asked as her heartbeat began to speed up. She stopped wrapping the antiques and looked at Free in concern.

"Oh, nothing, baby. Just can't be too careful," Free said, deciding not to worry her. They were about to move far away and he didn't feel the need to concern her over something that was probably nothing.

"Turn that up!" Free said as he glanced at the TV. Six picked up the remote and turned up CNN. There was a red flash across the screen. Michael Jackson had just died.

"Damn, Mike gone?" Lou asked in disbelief.

"Damn, I can't believe it," Six said as she put her hands on her hips. Free looked on in disbelief as he shook his head disappointedly.

"He was the best," Lou added.

Then another news flash popped up, saying that Britain "Brick" Adams had been exonerated from all charges concerning the big drug-trafficking case. CNN also mentioned the four federal agents who were killed and allegedly hit by the notorious Brick Adams. Free and Lou each looked at each other and smiled, knowing they were behind that massacre. They were the ones laughing in the end, because although Britain refused to pay them after the murders, they still got broke off, thanks to Six. Six smiled inside, knowing that Britain was okay and had beaten the case. She could now close that chapter of her life and move forward with Free.

# Chapter Twenty

Six looked around the clothing store that she owned and smiled in accomplishment. A year had passed since she had taken the money from Britain, and she and Free were doing well. They weren't living the life of the rich and famous. She had been there and done that with Britain. She never expected Free to be able to keep up with Brick's extraordinary lifestyle, but they were comfortable, and she was satisfied with that.

They had taken the money from the lick and moved out of Detroit, then opened up a few small businesses to legitimize their paper. Although she still could not bring herself to fully trust Free, they were working on their relationship. Her love for him never wavered, and she was so grateful to have her soul mate in her life. They belonged together, and although it took them being apart to find out that, they were more committed now than ever before.

Exhausted from a long day of work, she turned off the illuminated business light, letting her customers know that she was closed. Just as she locked the door, the handle jiggled on the other side.

"Sorry, we're closed!" she yelled as she walked away from the door.

"I can't wait to get to the crib," she mumbled as she grabbed her car keys and purse. Pulling out her cell phone, Six saw that she had two missed calls from Free. As she left the building, she fumbled with her belongings while she checked her voice mail.

"Hey, Six, it's me. Just wanted to check in with you to make sure everything's good. I'll be home in a couple days. I love you, ma. I've got a surprise for you when I get back."

Six pursed her lips as her eyebrows furrowed in suspicion. *He better not be out there clowning,* she thought as she opened up her text-message application to contact him.

    I CAN'T WAIT UNTIL YOU COME HOME

    I MISS YOU

    DON'T BE WILD'N OUT IN VEGAS, NIGGA

    I DON'T WANT TO HAVE TO FUCK A BITCH UP

    LOVE ALWAYS

    SIX

She threw her phone in her purse and headed to the parking lot. Six got into her car and pulled out into the Detroit traffic. Popping her Chrisette Michele into her CD player, she simultaneously pulled a pre-rolled blunt out of her ashtray to enjoy on the way home. She could feel the knock of her subwoofers vibrating through her seat as she nodded her head in unison to the beat and lit the la.

The lyrics to the song made her think about Free. She was lucky to have him in her life, and even though they had just been through hard times, she could see the light shining at the end of the tunnel. She would sacrifice herself for her man any day that he needed her to, and that's exactly what she had done. A fake chick would have left him high and dry when he was at his lowest, but Six was one of the few real ones. She stood by her man and did what she had to do to be his rock.

*I'm so glad that he's in my life. I would do anything for that nigga. He's my baby, and I love him.*

Her thoughts distracted her the entire way home. Relief washed over her when she finally pulled up to her crib. She hit the alarm on her car just before she walked into the house.

"Oh my God," she stated in shock as she looked around at the flickering candles that were burning inside her home. She dropped her purse, and a smile blessed her face. *Free thinks he slick. This must be the surprise he was talking about.*

"Free! Baby, why didn't you tell me you was coming home early?" she called out. She went into the kitchen and retrieved a bottle of wine, grabbing two flutes and pouring them as she walked up the stairs, her voluptuous ass moving from side to side. "You really outdid yourself, babe! I love all the candles," she said.

She walked into her bedroom and didn't see Free inside. Setting the glasses on the night-stand, she looked around in delight. Quickly she pulled her shirt over her head, leaving her in only a black Victoria Secrets bra and her skin-tight Skinny jeans with heels. Six pulled her hair out of the ponytail it was in and walked over to her vanity and took a seat. After spraying on perfume, she began to brush her hair. Suddenly the sound of R. Kelly crooned throughout the house, and she smiled when she heard footsteps coming up the stairs.

"Baby, come in here. I'ma put it on you tonight. . . . You earned it," she cooed seductively. She saw his reflection in the mirror. All she could see was his sexy midsection as he walked behind her. "Damn, baby, you been working out, nigga," she teased, noticing that the cuts in his stomach were more defined. He came near and when he was directly behind her he put his hands on her neck, causing her to close her eyes as he massaged gently. "That feels good."

His grip grew tighter, and Six winced in pain. "Damn, babe, that's kind of rough," she complained as she opened her eyes. Suddenly he leaned over in her ear, revealing his face in her mirror, and her eyes bucked in fear.

Her heart instantly collapsed into her stomach and a single tear slid down her cheek. She knew that she was in trouble; there was no way she was going to get out of this. Her fate was in his hands. She had crossed him, and she knew that he was not the forgiving type—in fact, he was the torturing type.

"What up, bitch? Guess who's back?" Twin asked menacingly through clenched teeth. A cloth-covered hand swiftly covered her mouth as he grabbed her in a chokehold and snatched her backward out of the chair. She could barely breathe as she tried to inch her fingers between his forearms to relieve the pressure around her windpipe.

"Ahhhh!" she screamed as she kicked and contorted her body in an effort to get away from him. Six smelled a strong chemical on the rag, and as she inhaled the strong vapor, her body became weak. She felt her eyelids close. *Please God,* was the last thought that crossed her mind before she slipped into unconsciousness.

Six's eyes opened slowly, and her head felt as if it weighed a thousand pounds as it fell to the side. The room spun as she tried to focus. She blinked her eyes lazily, trying to make everything come into clear vision, but nothing worked.

"Help me," she whispered.

"Nobody's coming, bitch," she heard Twin reply. "You thought you could get away from me . . . steal my money and run away with another nigga?" he asked, sounding like the devil himself.

Twin roughly snatched her jeans off of her body. He panted like a crazed dog, and Six tried to slap his hands away but her body was so weak. Her limbs felt so heavy that she could barely move her arms.

"What did you give me?" she uttered as she struggled. Twin laughed at her and ripped her panties to shreds.

"I've been waiting a long time for this, bitch. When you stole my money I looked all over the fucking city for you. Nobody had seen or heard from you until I saw you parading around on CNN with that nigga Brick. Imagine how good it felt when I was sitting at home minding my business and your face popped on the TV screen," Twin stated as he began to unbuckle his belt.

"Aghh," Six moaned as her eyes rolled back in her head. Her body was not her own, and she could not control her reflexes. She knew that whatever he had drugged her with was deadly. She could feel the strength leaving her body. Twin smacked her across the face, and Six's head twirled in the direction of the hit. Her neck was like noodles as she pushed at Twin, uselessly wrestling to get him off of her. She was so high that even her tongue felt numb and she had a hard time even forming the words to protest.

"I've been on you for the past year. Watching your every move," Twin stated as he took one of the wax candles and spread the lips of her vagina, pouring the melted hotness all over her clit.

Six's eyes bulged out of her head in horrendous pain, but all she could do was moan and arch her back slightly. *Please God, help me. He is going to kill me,* she prayed. Six closed her eyes and inhaled slowly, trying to calm the burning sensation between her legs as Twin continued to talk.

"It's been hard to get close to you, Six. You always had somebody around you. The one time I thought I had you, I snuck into your house, but you weren't home. . . . But guess who was home, Six?" he asked as he kneeled beside her so that they were face-to-face.

The sight of Twin disgusted Six, and she used all of her remaining strength to spit in his face. Twin calmly wiped the saliva out of his eyes and smiled. "Your father fought back the same way, bitch, but that didn't stop me from killing him either. You're gonna die tonight."

Tears flooded Six's eyes when she heard that Twin had murdered her father. "Why?" she asked as the tears rolled down her cheeks and her head lay limply on the bed.

"Why?" Twin asked mockingly. "Because you crossed me and revenge is sweet. You ruined my fucking life over that money, bitch. I owed that paper to a nigga, and when I couldn't pay up, he took my debt out on my moms and my sister. So that's why. You signed your own death certificate when you took my money."

He began to remove his jeans while staring lustfully at Six. She could see from the look in his deranged stare that he had a horrible death in mind for her. She wanted to tell him that she would give him back the money. She wanted to say that she was sorry for what she did, but as her drug-induced fatigue grew stronger, she could not bring herself to speak. Her world went white as her eyes continued to roll in the back of her head.

"First, I'ma wear this pussy out. It's been a long time, Six. You might as well kiss the devil before he takes your life," Twin stated. He climbed on top of her and roughly pried her legs open, then shoved himself forcefully inside.

"Ow," Six whimpered as her head rolled weakly to the side and her eyes continued to roll around in her head. "Please stop," she cried weakly.

Twin raped Six and in his mind her whimpers sounded like moans of pleasure. As he looked down into her face, he could see that she was high out of her mind. The combination of heroin and rat poison he had given her was slowly torturing her. He smiled as he saw her pupils turn completely white and her mouth fall open. Twin continued to sex her as his moans of passion filled the room.

*Focus, Six!* she urged herself as she felt Twin moving in and out of her, stabbing her to death with his tool. She opened her eyes and out of the corner of her eye she could see a shadow reflecting off of the walls as someone moved in the hallway. *Free!* she thought frantically. *Please, baby, I need you!* her mind screamed. She opened her mouth to call out to him, but the only sounds that came out were moans and grunts. Twin was so busy humping away that he didn't notice that someone else was creeping into the room. Six reached out her hand just as Free entered the room.

"Ahhhh," she cried out as tears ran down her cheeks. For a split second Free paused in shock as his eyes met hers. He took in the scene before him, and she could see the hurt in his eyes as he misinterpreted the scene before him. She tried to make her lips move to call out to him.

*Free, help me!*

"Bitch, you fucking this nigga?" he screamed as he pulled out his pistol from his waistline.

*No, Free, don't! Please, it's not what it looks like!* she screamed in her head.

*Pow, pow, pow!*

He loaded Twin up as he approached the bed enraged, the bullets sending Twin flying off of Six. Tears poured from his eyes as he witnessed the woman he loved more than anything fucking another man. He snapped as his adrenaline sent him into a crazed rage.

"Bitch, you fucking this nigga?" he asked again as he approached her. Six stared up into Free's eyes as tears rolled down her face.

*Please, Free, no!* she thought desperately as she closed her eyes.

"I loved you, ma . . . you love this nigga?" Free asked, crying hysterically as he stared down at Six. He wiped his nose and said, "I'm not giving you to another nigga. I love you too much, ma."

Six opened her eyes. *Talk . . . say something!* she thought. She watched helplessly as Free loomed over her with the gun. Her lips quivered as tried to speak. "Free," she whispered desperately.

Free leaned over, his tears wetting her face as he kissed her cheeks. There was so much red on the sheets from where Free had blown Twin away. Blood on Free's hands . . . blood on his shirt, his shoes, blood in his eyes. The sound of his heart breaking could be heard only by Six as her eyes pleaded with him.

He kissed her once. "I love you, Six."

He kissed her twice. "Forever," he stated.

He put the trigger to her temple—bang!

Then turned it on himself—bang!

Kiss! Kiss! Bang! Bang! It was the ceremony he performed before he took his own life. It was the most complicated love story ever told.

# Epilogue

*Three Weeks Later*

A pulsating pain shot through Six's body as she slowly opened her eyes. The room was dark, and she was unaware of her surroundings. *Beep, beep, beep, beep!* The steady tone of the machines around her was all that could be heard. The small sound seemed so loud inside her head. Each beep made a sharp explosion go off inside her brain, causing her great pain. Her eyes darted wildly around the room as she searched for something familiar. *Where am I? What happened?* she thought frantically as she tried to move her body. Her lungs felt deprived for air as she struggled to breathe deeply. She wanted to sit up, she wanted to scream for help, but her body would not cooperate. No matter how hard she tried, she was unable to move. Her throat felt like it was on fire, and her heart rate increased dramatically as fear gripped her body. *Beep,*

*beep, beep, beep!* The sound of the machines intensified, and she heard the sound of people rushing into her room.

"Is she all right? What's happening to her?" Six heard Big Lou's voice, and her eyes scanned the many faces that were surrounding her bed as she tried to locate him.

"I'm sorry, sir, you have to wait outside. You can see her once we've stabilized her."

"Is she okay? Just tell me what's happening!" she heard Big Lou demand, his voice frantic with worry.

"Free!" she cried out. His voice was the only voice that she didn't hear. He was the one that she needed right now. *Where is he?*

"I need her calm. Her body is in shock," one of the doctors instructed. Six watched as a young nurse filled a syringe with fluid and injected it into her arm.

"No! Free—I want to see Free!" Six cried in a raspy tone. Her voice was almost inaudible. Her body was weak, but she still fought against the hospital staff as she begged to see her man.

"Look at my hand and count down with me," a doctor stated.

"Five, four, three, two . . ." before he even got to *one* Six felt her eyelids close involuntarily, taking her to a temporary sanctuary of peace.

\*\*\*

Six opened her eyes and immediately sensed the figure who was sitting in the chair beside her bed. She couldn't move her head to see who it was, but she could feel him watching her.

"Free," she whispered, her voice cracking.

"Free's not here, Six. It's me, Big Lou," he whispered as he stood up so that she could see him. "You had me worried for a minute, sis."

"Where is Free? What happened to me? I feel like I can't breathe. Why isn't he here?" she asked.

"You don't remember anything? You don't remember what happened?" Big Lou asked her in bewilderment.

"No, where is he, Lou?"

Before Big Lou could respond, a middle-aged black man entered the room. He was wearing a long lab coat with blue scrubs underneath. Big Lou was grateful for the interruption. He didn't know how to tell Six that Free was dead.

"Six Jones," the doctor stated as he walked up to her bed. He took off his stethoscope and placed the cold metal to her chest. "You are a very lucky young woman."

"What happened to me?" she asked the doctor. The doctor's face immediately expressed confusion as he looked toward Big Lou.

"She doesn't remember," Big Lou answered the doctor's question before he could even ask it.

"Well, Ms. Jones . . ." the doctor started. He was hesitant to inform her of her condition. "You were shot in the head. You are extremely lucky to be alive. That's why you are having such a hard time moving and breathing. During the shooting, a part of your brain called the cerebellum was injured. A part of the brain stem that controls your breathing was also injured. The massive head trauma that you have sustained has caused you to become immobile."

"I'm paralyzed?" Six whispered with tears in her eyes. She stared up toward the ceiling as she tried to process what the doctor was telling her.

"Not exactly. The damage is not permanent. But your body has to learn how to function again. That's why you are hooked up to the breathing machine. Your brain is not sending the correct signals to the rest of your body. You can't breathe or move on your own yet."

"Where is Free? I need him?" she said as her tears began to flow. She gasped for air, struggling to breathe.

"She doesn't know?" the doctor asked as he looked toward Big Lou again.

"I can't tell her, yo," Big Lou said as he gripped Six's hand and tears began to well in his own eyes.

"Tell me what?" she asked. "Where is he? Big Lou, where is Free?"

The doctor excused himself so that he could give them some privacy.

"Six, he's gone. He shot you, then he turned the gun on himself."

Six didn't respond. She stared at Big Lou as tears streamed endlessly down her face. *He can't be gone. He told me he would never leave me. Why would he do this to me? Free, I need you.* Her body shuddered as she thought about the death of Free. He had been her best friend and her heart. She couldn't find any words to describe how she felt; her heart was numb.

She closed her eyes, and images of Free entered her mind. The entire scene instantly came back to her as she played it back in her head. She could hear the blast from the gun in her ears. She could feel his pain as he asked her repeatedly, *Do you love this nigga? Do you love this nigga?* Six saw the spark from the barrel of the gun as Free pulled the trigger. "Oh my God! Big Lou! Oh God! He can't be gone. I can't do this without him. I need him," she cried. Tears of despair stained her cheeks as she lay helplessly in the hospital bed. "How did this happen? Where is he? Big Lou—"

"He's gone, Six . . . he's gone," Big Lou said as he held her hand.

"I just want to be alone," she stated as she closed her eyes.

Big Lou nodded slowly. "All right. I'll be right outside if you need me."

"Big Lou . . . when is his funeral?" Six asked before he stepped out.

"You've been in a coma for the past three weeks. The funeral was two weeks ago." He waited for her to reply, but when she didn't, he walked out of the room.

She couldn't stop the tears from escaping from her eyes. She was deeply hurt by Free's death. Her soul ached unbearably as she tried to imagine her life without him in it. *How did we get here? How did I let this happen?* Six stared at the ceiling and gripped her bedsheets as she thought about her tragic lost.

She heard the door open, but she closed her eyes to avoid being bothered. "I just want to be left alone," she said.

"I want to leave you alone, ma, but there's something about you that keeps calling me back."

Six's eyes shot open in disbelief when she heard his voice. "Britain?" she stated with a quiver as she looked at him as if he might disappear before her eyes.

"Yeah, it's me . . . shh, just relax. You don't have to say anything. I'm here," he replied as he grabbed an ice cube out of the bucket on the nightstand and placed it to her chapped lips.

Six stared into his eyes. Nothing about him had changed. It had been over a year since she had last seen him. The last time they had interacted she had crossed him, but there was no larceny in his heart. His gaze was still as loving and gentle toward her as it had always been.

"Why are you here?" she whispered.

"Because I love you," he answered. "Money can be replaced, Six—you cannot. I'm just upset that it had to come to this for me to realize that. I should have never let you walk out my door. I would have kept you safe."

Six didn't know how to respond to him. He was so forgiving. . . . Any woman would be lucky to call herself his lady, but Six belonged to Free. Britain was just a beautiful distraction and a horrible mistake. She had stolen his heart without giving hers to him in return.

"I'm sorry," she stated.

"I once told you that no matter what happened between us I would make sure you were straight. I didn't do that, Six. I broke my word to you. I won't do it again. I know you loved Free, but he's the reason you're sitting in this bed hanging onto your life. Let me take care of you. Let me keep my word this time around," he stated.

Six gave him a weak smile, but they were interrupted when a nurse walked into the room.

"I'm sorry, sir, but visiting hours are over," she stated.

Britain leaned over and kissed Six's cheek. "I'm coming back for you," he whispered. "Get some rest. I'll be here in the morning. I love you."

"I love you too," she whispered back.

When Britain walked out of the room Six cried as her life's circumstances haunted her. Now was her chance to move on with Britain, but in her heart, she knew that she could never let go of Free. Yes, it was true that she did love Britain, but her feelings for Free were so much deeper than love. They were soul mates, and even though Free was no longer living, Six could still feel his energy. She was in love with Free. She was linked to him in a way that didn't allow her to invest herself into anyone else.

Six heard the hum of the machines that surrounded her, keeping her alive, then she pictured Free's face. Britain could be a lovely substitute, but Free was the one who she belonged to . . . who she belonged with.

"If you die, I die," she whispered, remembering something that she had told him a long time ago to show her loyalty. Six inhaled deeply as she thought of what she was about to do. She used all of her will to lift her arm. It trembled rapidly as pain shot through her body, but Six didn't stop until her hand was wrapped around the oxygen tube that was inserted into her nose. She remembered the doctor's words.

*Your body has to learn how to function again. That's why you are hooked up to the breathing machine. Your brain is not sending the correct signals to the rest of your body. You can't breathe or move on your own.*

"Aghh!" Six whimpered as she tugged at the oxygen tube, yanking it from her nose.

Six's body immediately went into convulsions as she struggled to inhale. She knew that she was committing suicide and the temporary pain she was feeling would soon disappear. She jerked violently and the monitors beeped like crazy as the hospital staff hurried into her room. They were too late, however. Six felt her soul drifting away as the convulsions died down.

*I love you, Free. I'm on my way to you,* she thought.

The heart monitor flat lined indicating that Six was no longer alive. The doctor shook his head as he looked at the room clock.

"Time of death . . . eleven twenty-eight P.M."